RDED

ED

D1262494

SPECIAL MESSAGE TO READERS

This book is published under the auspices of

THE ULVERSCROFT FOUNDATION

(registered charity No. 264873 UK)

Established in 1972 to provide funds for research, diagnosis and treatment of eye diseases. Examples of contributions made are: —

A Children's Assessment Unit at
Moorfield's Hospital, London.

•

Twin operating theatres at the
Western Ophthalmic Hospital, London.

•

A Chair of Ophthalmology at the
Royal Australian College of Ophthalmologists.

•

The Ulverscroft Children's Eye Unit at the
Great Ormond Street Hospital For Sick Children,
London.

You can help further the work of the Foundation by making a donation or leaving a legacy. Every contribution, no matter how small, is received with gratitude. Please write for details to:

THE ULVERSCROFT FOUNDATION,
The Green, Bradgate Road, Anstey,
Leicester LE7 7FU, England.
Telephone: (0116) 236 4325

In Australia write to:
THE ULVERSCROFT FOUNDATION,
c/o The Royal Australian and New Zealand
College of Ophthalmologists,
94-98, Chalmers Street, Surry Hills,
N.S.W. 2010, Australia

FOREVER IN MY HEART

With the support of a loving family, Julie Haywood is coping well with the trauma of divorce and the difficulties of single parenthood. Well on track with her medical career, she is looking forward to an exciting new promotion — not realising it will bring her into contact with Rob, a part of her past she has tried to forget. Then, when ex-husband Geoff turns up, Julie finds she has some hard decisions to make . . .

Bruce County Public Library
1243 Mackenzie Rd.
Port Elgin ON N0H 2C6

Books by Joyce Johnson
in the Linford Romance Library:

ROUGH MAGIC
BITTER INHERITANCE
HOSTAGES OF FATE
SWEET LEGACY
DARK SECRET
THE SILKEN SNARE
CHANGING FORTUNES
JOURNEY INTO DANGER
TO WIN HER LOVE
SUMMER DREAM
LOVING PIONEERS
DANGEROUS LEGACY
HERITAGE OF LOVE
LOST HEART
FOR LOVE OF AN ISLAND
IN THE LIMELIGHT
LOVE ON THE MOOR
DANGEROUS JOURNEY
DARK SHADOWS
LOVE AND WAR
HIDDEN MEMORIES
DECEPTION
LOVE'S LOST TREASURE
SUSPICIOUS HEART
EDEN IN PARADISE
SWEET CHALLENGE

JOYCE JOHNSON

FOREVER IN MY HEART

Complete and Unabridged

LINFORD
Leicester

First published in Great Britain in 2007

First Linford Edition
published 2007

Copyright © 2007 by Joyce Johnson
All rights reserved

British Library CIP Data

Johnson, Joyce, *1931* –
    Forever in my heart.—Large print ed.—
Linford romance library
1. Divorced mothers—Fiction 2. Triangles
(Interpersonal relations)—Fiction
3. Love stories 4. Large type books
I. Title
823.9'2 [F]

ISBN 978–1–84617–987–7

Published by
F. A. Thorpe (Publishing)
Anstey, Leicestershire

Set by Words & Graphics Ltd.
Anstey, Leicestershire
Printed and bound in Great Britain by
T. J. International Ltd., Padstow, Cornwall

This book is printed on acid-free paper

Time To Celebrate

Julie Haywood checked her appearance in the full-length mirror. Her aim was to look cool and confident. She ignored the butterflies in her stomach, knowing that they were necessary to produce the adrenaline she needed to face an audience. She tucked a rogue lock of hair behind her ear, adjusted the set of her fine wool jacket and took a deep breath. Mentally scrolling through her notes and figures, confident that she had a clear grasp of her material, she made her way to the conference hall.

As she entered the hall, the buzz of conversation faded. Eric Lancaster, head of Maldon's Pharmaceutical Research and her immediate boss, smiled encouragement from the dais. She joined him and nodded to the audience, recognising several of her former colleagues from the maternity department of St Clements Hospital; it was just what she needed to spur her on to do well.

'Julie Haywood is well known to several of you,' Eric Lancaster announced. 'She may even have delivered some of your babies before she joined our team. We're very glad that she did. Julie is doing valuable research work, liaising with medical teams in the area. This afternoon she is opening our two-day conference with a presentation on Seasonal Affective Disorder, part of a wider study on depression which Maldon's is researching.' He stepped back and repeated, 'Julie Haywood.'

As Julie stepped forward, her heart was pounding, but outwardly she showed no sign of nerves. As she reached the dais, her wide smile was so infectious that most of the audience instinctively smiled back.

'Thank you.' Her clear voice carried to all corners. 'You see how easy it is to catch a smile? A smile can lift a mood, just as spring sunshine can tweak aside the dark blackout of winter for people who suffer from S.A.D. But as we all know, sunshine is unreliable, especially in our unpredictable climate, so at Maldon's we're working on ways to replicate natural sunshine. Today I'd like to show you our interim results and future pathways . . . '

She began to enjoy herself as she worked through her material. She had the full attention of her audience, several of whom were taking notes and forty minutes later, as she began to wind up her presentation, she knew she'd done a good job.

'To sum up, I believe prospects are good . . . ' She paused as a latecomer slipped quietly into a seat at the back. 'I . . . er . . . but I . . . ' She coughed, her chain of thought shattered. 'Sorry.'

She sipped some water, willing herself to concentrate, and with a deep breath, she managed to finish as planned: 'Finally then, as you can see, there's still work to be done.'

She embraced her audience with a

smile, gathering up her notes to a round of applause. She couldn't help stealing a glance to the back of the hall. He was still there, the latecomer, now standing talking to a grey-haired man she recognised as a leading professor of obstetrics and gynaecology at London University. For a split second the younger man turned towards her and she saw him frown, but someone else joined them just then and all three turned to leave the hall.

Julie shook her head. Of course it wasn't him! She hadn't seen him or even thought about him for years . . . but the resemblance had unnerved her.

'Julie, that was excellent!' Eric Lancaster beamed as he shook her hand. 'Hit the nail right on the head. Let me buy you a drink — the bar's just about to open.'

'I'd like that, Eric,' she replied, 'but I'm due at Professor Rutherford's retirement party. I promised to pop in.'

'Maybe tomorrow then?'

'I hope so. I'm glad it went well.'

'It did. You got us off to a good start. Some other time then, for that drink.' He gave her a pat on the shoulder. 'Good work, Julie, you've done well. Time to move you on.'

'Move on? But . . . '

'Move up, I should say, but I won't keep you now. We aren't involved in the conference until tomorrow afternoon so — first thing in the morning, my office. Now, I must run and catch Professor . . . '

'But . . . '

'Julie, could you clarify a point?' Mark Goodman, a consultant psychiatrist at St Clements, caught her attention and was soon joined by other members of his team. Julie enjoyed these personal contacts which her new job involved and was soon deep in conversation with her former St Clements' colleagues until a glance at her watch told her she was cutting things fine for time.

'Sorry, guys, I really must run.

E-mail me with any queries and I'll get back to you. Thanks for being such a good audience.'

As she hurried towards the exit, she caught a glimpse of the tall, dark stranger who'd come into the hall so late. He was in front of her so she quickened her step, but he turned off before she managed to catch up with him. It *couldn't* be Rob Kendall! But she was startled to find that even a passing resemblance to him could bring a flush of embarrassment to her face.

It was quite ridiculous; she hadn't even thought of Rob for years. Besides, she bore no relation to that poor gauche teenager of over a decade ago; she was a completely different person now, in a completely different life. She pushed away the unsettling fragment of memory from the past and concentrated on the present.

She was obliged to put in a brief appearance at the professor's leaving do, then she was off to her sister Olivia's.

Olivia should know the results of her tests by now and would be on her way home from London. Julie took out her mobile and dialled her sister's number but it came back 'unavailable'. She checked her own messages — nothing. She frowned. It could be a bad sign, but then again, her older sister was rarely predictable — she'd probably forgotten to switch on her phone.

Party noise greeted her as she entered the staff-room. One of her friends, Valerie Boone, rushed over to greet her.

'Thank goodness! I thought you were going to miss it. The prof's been asking for you.'

'Really? What for?'

'He's fond of you, that's why. You were part of his team for years.'

'Thanks. You make me sound ancient,' said Julie with a laugh.

'Ah, Julie, my dear.' Professor Rutherford's bulky form pushed through the crowd. 'I'm so glad you made it. How was the conference?'

'Off to a good start, thanks. It went well.'

'I'm glad the job's working out, but you're a great loss to us. Best maternity sister I ever had.'

'Thank you. I do miss this though.' She looked around as more and more people squeezed into the crowded room, some coming on shift in working uniforms, others dressed to leave for the outside world.

'I'm going to get the surprise cake,' Val hissed in her ear. 'Keep the old chap talking.'

The noise level was becoming deafening. Julie did her best to speak to the professor but he shook his head, pointing to his hearing aid.

'These things aren't much use in this sort of situation — too much background noise. But I'm grateful for the party,' he shouted, smiling. Then he leaned closer. 'I'd just like to say I'm not leaving the country. Kathy and I intend to travel but we'll never leave the Dales for good. We're both very fond of you, you know, so you must come and visit often, have supper, keep us in touch with the real world.'

'I'd love to,' Julie responded.

He gave her a hug before being swallowed up by a crowd of admirers.

Valerie appeared at her elbow. 'You have to stay for the cake, it's coming in a minute. Glasses are being refilled.'

Julie shook her head. 'I really can't, much as I'd like to. Who's coming as the prof's replacement?'

'Some whizz-kid from Australia. Starts next week. Polly's livid, but Dan's pleased. He didn't fancy Polly as his boss.'

Mouthing 'Bye', Julie pointed to her watch.

'OK. There's a new club in town,' Val shouted. 'We're going next weekend. Join us.'

'I'll see. I'll ring you.'

Val sighed. She knew it would all depend on Olivia and whether she would require her younger sister at the weekend. Val, a local girl, knew the

Balboni family well and had noticed Olivia demanding more and more of what little free time Julie had.

⋆　⋆　⋆

On the way to the car park Julie took out her mobile again and rang her mother's phone number. It rang for ages, and by the time she reached her car, she was worried. Tim should have been home from school ages ago. It was a Wednesday, not a football, tennis or swimming day.

She was about to leave a message when her mother's breathless voice answered: 'Julie! I'm here.'

'Is Tim with you?'

'Of course. I picked him up a couple of hours ago, but Sam and Eddie popped by, so we've been kicking a football around the garden. Is everything all right?'

'Yes, fine. I'm just running a bit late, and I'm going on to Olivia's.'

'Ah. It was the clinic today?'

'Yes, and she wants me to be there when she gets home. You know Michael's in Dubai . . . ' There was a pause. 'Mum? Are you still there?'

'Yes. Give her my love. Let me know the test results . . . '

Another pregnant pause.

'What, Mum? What's the problem?'

'Julie, don't be too late home. I'm happy to oversee Tim's homework, but he asked how late you'd be tonight. You've hardly seen him all week.'

Guilt pricked Julie. 'Oh, Mum, I'm sorry. I know I've missed his bedtime lately but the conference . . . I had to work on my talk. Tell Tim I'll be back as soon as I can — but you know what Olivia's like. And she needs me right now. If the results are negative again . . . '

'I know, but Tim needs you, too — and he's your son. Olivia is your sister, she's ten years older than you *and* she's got a husband.' The situation had obviously been worrying Sandra Balboni for some time.

'But . . .'

Sandra broke in: 'I must go. I promised chips for tea and they'll be burned to a frazzle. See you soon.'

Julie replaced her phone in her bag and rummaged for her car keys. It was true, Olivia relied on her too much. That was part of family history. Tim should be — *was* — her priority, but he was such an easy little boy compared with Olivia.

She pressed the keypad to open the car door, and jumped as an arm went round her shoulders.

'Julie.'

'Dan. Hi! I missed you at the party.'

'Sorry, I had to help out at Woodlands — a private patient of Rutherford's.' Dan Foster was a senior registrar at St Clements and one of Julie's best friends.

'There's a lively party over at St Clements,' she told him.

'So I hear. I'm on my way now. Surely you're not leaving? I haven't seen you for ages and I was hoping for a chat. How's the new job?'

'Fine. I'm enjoying it.'

'We miss you in the department. It hasn't been the same since you left.'

'Nonsense. Anyway, the new consultant replacing the prof will probably shake you up — he's a live-wire, I hear.'

Dan grimaced. 'Do we need a live-wire? Polly's very aggrieved that she's been passed over. The new guy will find her a hard nut.'

'She'll get over it . . . Hey, look out, Dan!'

Dan leapt out of the path of a car speeding its way to the car park exit.

'He came out of Maternity. Maybe he's in a hurry to spread the good news of son and heir,' he mused.

'He'll be lucky if he gets there alive, driving at that speed! Did you recognise him?'

'No. So if I can't persuade you to come back to the party with me, I may just pop in and say hello and goodbye to the professor.'

'You're sure you don't know the guy

in that car?' Julie pressed.

'I don't think so, but I only got a glimpse. Why are you so curious?'

'Oh, nothing. Forget it.' Julie reached up to kiss him on the cheek. 'Take care, Dan. I miss you, too.'

'Why don't I come over one evening next week and we can take Tim bowling?'

'Oh, Dan, would you? He'd love that!'

'Me, too. I'll ring you.'

Julie stood by her car as Dan went on his way. That third glimpse of the dark stranger in the car worried her. The last she'd heard of Rob Kendall, he'd been doing heroic things in Europe with Medecins Sans Frontieres. And hadn't he vowed never to return to small-town life in the Yorkshire Dales?

She shook her head and unlocked her car. Next stop, Olivia's house and a prayer for the news to be good.

★ ★ ★

As she drove across town towards the more affluent suburbs of Royston, Julie thought about her sister. If it was bad news, she had to be there to pick up the pieces.

If only Michael was home more often to give Olivia support. Granted, he made wads of money from his debenture work, enough to provide Olivia with every material comfort, an immaculately-furnished executive-style home and a live-in housekeeper to maintain it.

Julie turned into the double gates guarding a manicured drive, to be met by a frenzy of barking as two Labradors rushed out of the house to meet the car.

'Hi, you two.' She laughed as they nosed her pockets for the biscuits they knew she always carried for them. 'Here you are, Petra. You too, Jake. Now, where's your mistress? Let's find her.'

She followed them into the house. The spacious hall was sunlit but empty and Julie's worries resurfaced. Olivia had surely heard the dogs and the car.

So it had to be bad news — Olivia must be curled up in a ball somewhere, sobbing in disappointment.

Julie breathed again as a cheerful voice came from the stairs.

'Hi, Julie! Sorry — I was in the shower.' Wrapped in a white towelling bathrobe, Olivia came on to the upper landing and leaned over the stair rail. 'Lovely to see you. I'm coming down.'

Julie's heart flipped at the radiant smile on her older sister's face.

'It's . . . is it . . . ?' She daren't say it, there had been so many disappointments in the past years.

'Yes!' Olivia ran down the stairs and flung her arms round Julie. 'I'm pregnant!' she shouted. 'Pregnant — at long last. Isn't it wonderful?'

'I'm so happy for you.' Julie hugged her, and the dogs, catching the moment, started barking again, and for a few seconds there was pandemonium. Olivia started to cry and Julie felt near to tears herself.

'Come on, sit down. Tell me all about

it,' she said. 'Is it certain?'

'Yes. They were great at the clinic — almost as pleased as I am.'

'Well, it's their success story, too. You've been with them quite a while.'

'I can't take it in! After all this time, since losing baby Sarah . . . '

'Don't think about that. That's the past. Think about the future now. You get dressed and I'll make us some tea. Have you eaten?'

'I bought a sandwich on the train but it nearly choked me.'

'I'll put the kettle on and see what's in the fridge.'

'There's champagne in the fridge. I put it in the moment I got home.'

Julie looked doubtful. 'Is that wise?'

'Half a glass won't hurt me, and I promise it'll be the last sip of alcohol until . . . ' she put her hands on her stomach ' . . . he or she is born.'

'Have you told Michael?'

'He's out of town — some desert jamboree. I left a message at his hotel to phone.'

'I was worried when you didn't phone me.'

'I tried from London but the network was down, then I lost my mobile on the train — but you will stay? Please?'

Julie waggled her head. 'I can't stay long. Where's Ellena?'

'Ellena?' Olivia frowned. 'Er — what day is it?'

'Thursday.'

'It's her day off . . . I think.'

'Don't you know?'

'Oh, she comes and goes all the time. I don't know,' Olivia said vaguely.

'Don't you talk to her?'

'What about?' Olivia looked astonished. 'She does the work, she's a good cook. In fact, Michael prefers her cooking to mine — when he's home, that is.'

'When will he be back?'

'A few days, I think. Look, you must stay the night. I'm so excited I'll never sleep. We can have lots of champagne and then . . . '

'*You* won't,' Julie reminded her.

'Oh, no, of course not. I forgot. How could I?' She went into the kitchen and pulled a bottle out the fridge. 'Here — you open it.'

'Shouldn't you have something to eat first? And I still don't think even half a glass of champagne's a good idea.'

'Oh, don't be such a spoilsport. Don't you understand? *I am pregnant.* A baby at last.'

Reluctantly Julie opened the champagne, took two glasses from a cupboard, half filled one and poured a very small amount in the other.

'Julie, for heaven's sake!' Olivia grasped the bottle, poured a splash more into her glass and filled Julie's to the top.

'But I'm driving!' Julie protested.

'But you can't go back tonight. You must stay. I don't want to be on my own.'

'I have to get back. Can't you call a friend? Molly? Lucy?'

'No, no, it's family I need. Anyway, Lucy's abroad and Molly goes to the gym every night.'

'You used to go with her, didn't you?'

'Yes, but it got boring, and anyway, I can't now, can I?'

'Why not? There are special pre-natal classes at St Clements. I can arrange . . . '

'Oh, not now,' Olivia interrupted impatiently. 'I can have my own personal trainer. Nothing must go wrong this time. I couldn't bear to lose this one, after Sarah . . . '

'Nothing will go wrong, I'm sure. We'll all help. Baby Sarah was just too premature to survive.'

'She would have been nine this month, on the thirteenth. Can you believe it? And it's been so hard since.' Olivia sipped her champagne. 'Trying to conceive, endless disappointments, all the treatments, persuading Michael to keep going. I thought I'd go mad. All my friends forever popping out new babies. I felt so hopeless . . . '

To Julie's alarm, Olivia began to cry, huge sobs shaking her shoulders.

'Olivia, please don't. You're upsetting yourself. Calm down.'

'I . . . I can't.' Olivia tugged tissues out of a box, scrunching them up to her eyes.

Julie had seen her sister in this state of near-hysteria many times and it had got worse each time the I.V.F. failed. Olivia was extremely highly-strung. There was a ten-year gap between her and the eldest of her three siblings, and Julie, Sam and Eddie had always been nervous of her moods. Yet she could be great fun, too — mercurial, storm and sunshine. Of the four of them, she was the only one to inherit the explosive Mediterranean temperament of their Italian father, Carlo Balboni.

Olivia's sobs continued and the dogs padded round her anxiously, making whining sounds. Julie took the champagne glass from her.

'Come on, you've got nothing to cry about. You're pregnant at last, it's what you've always wanted. And all this is bad for the baby.'

'Is it? Why didn't you tell me?'

'I didn't get a chance. You've had a hard day, I should have gone with you.'

'No, I was fine at the clinic. It's just reaction, I suppose, coming home, no-one here and . . . Julie, I think I was frightened, too — and I couldn't reach Michael. I'm sorry.'

'Don't be. Just dry your eyes and get dressed. I'll make the supper and you can try Michael again. What's the time difference in Dubai?'

'I'm not sure. Please don't leave me. I need you.'

'So does Tim.' Julie echoed her mother's words.

'Tim has Mum, Sam, Eddie, and their current girlfriends. He's got loads of people around him.'

'He still needs his own mother — and he's getting lots of homework now he's going to secondary school next year. I need to be there for him.'

'Yes, I know. I'm sorry, but it's lonely here, and so many of my friends have families.'

'You'll soon have yours. Why don't you come home with me tonight?'

'No, I won't, thanks. Michael will probably ring and there are the dogs, and Ellena will be in later. Just stay until she comes. Please, Ju.'

'I'll do supper, then we'll see.'

While Olivia dressed and fed the dogs, Julie made ham omelettes and salad which they ate at the kitchen breakfast bar. Olivia was calmer now, and with her long dark hair scraped back from her face, which was devoid of make-up, she looked younger and more vulnerable, and Julie felt a surge of protective love for her.

'I'm really pleased for you, Olivia. Hey, I'll be an aunt — my first niece or nephew.'

'No — Sarah was your first,' Olivia said sharply. 'You mustn't forget her — any of you.'

'Of course we won't. Olivia, you must promise to keep calm and do exactly what your doctor and midwife tell you.'

Olivia put her head in her hands. 'I'm

scared. What if . . . '

'Shush, nothing's going to happen. You'll be fine.'

Julie put their plates in the dishwasher.

'Now, I really must go. I promised.'

'Just a little while longer. There's still coffee in the pot.' Quickly Olivia poured Julie more coffee and then hesitated over her own. 'Should I be drinking coffee? And what sort of food . . . ?'

'You'll get all the advice you need at the clinic, and you'll find it fun meeting all the other mums.'

But Olivia persisted in questioning Julie and it was another hour before she finally left for home. Ellena had returned from her day off, so at least there was someone else there — as well as the Labradors.

*　*　*

Julie had to cross town to get back to the large family home where she and her son, Tim, lived in a self-contained

24

flat on the third floor. Traffic was light but there were one or two hold-ups and it was well past ten o'clock before she parked her car in the drive. She recognised her younger brother Sam's car in the drive. He was probably with Jane, his latest girlfriend.

She let herself in quietly and was on her way up to the flat when the sitting-room door opened.

'Hi, Julie, where've you been? Tim's been anxious.' Sam was a couple of years younger than Julie. He and his twin brother, Eddie, were as unalike in appearance as twins could be, but the bond between them — between all of them — was strong. He came forward to hug her. 'It's good to see you. Jane's here. We've been playing Monopoly with Tim. He's a whizz at it — a budding entrepreneur. What's the news of Olivia?'

'She's pregnant — at last.'

'That's great news. So I'll be an uncle. Does Mum know? She didn't say anything.'

'I've only just heard, that's why I'm late. Olivia said she needed me to stay with her.'

'Ah, at last.' Sandra Balboni, a plump, pretty woman in her late fifties, emerged from the sitting-room to kiss her daughter. 'Tim's so disappointed you didn't get back. I let him stay up late but he's asleep now.'

'Sorry, Mum, but Olivia got herself into a state and . . . '

'So what's new? But it was clinic day today. Poor Olivia — I expect it was bad news again?'

'No, she's pregnant. She's going to phone you.'

'Well!' Sandra sank down on the sofa. 'How wonderful! I never thought . . . But why was she upset? Surely this is exactly what she wants?'

'Oh, it's just reaction. And there was no-one in the house, so I . . . I just felt I had to stay a bit. Sorry.'

'You did the right thing, love. I'll phone her now. Oh, how did your day go? Wasn't it your big presentation today?'

'It seems a long time ago, but it went fine. Thanks for asking.' Impulsively Julie hugged the older woman. 'And thanks for looking after Tim.'

'No trouble, he's a lovely boy.'

While his mother dialled Olivia's number, Sam grinned at his sister.

'I'll break out the champagne. You look as though you need it!'

'Yes, I think I do. It's been a long day.'

Where Is Tim?

'Tim, wake up, we're late!' Julie yanked the duvet off her son's bed, ignoring his groans of protest as he fought to keep it wrapped around him. 'No . . . bathroom, quickly. Come on, Tim, I need to be early for work. Mr Lancaster wants to see me.'

'Isn't he the boss? I hope he's not going to sack you.'

'Of course he isn't. Up, up . . . '

'OK.' Tim yawned and rubbed his eyes. 'You were late back last night. I wanted you to see my history project — Romans in Britain.'

'I'm sorry, love. Tonight — I promise. I had to visit Aunt Olivia — and guess what? She's expecting a baby, a cousin for you.'

'Cool. I don't have any cousins, do I? Liam's got lots — most of them live around here.'

'You've got Italian cousins, Bianca and Angelo.'

'Grandpa Carlo's children? They're not really cousins, are they, and we hardly ever see them.'

'You're related. Perhaps we should visit them more often.'

Julie felt a pang of guilt. She loved her father, Carlo Balboni, but he had left his Yorkshire family ten years ago to marry Isabella, a young Italian girl from his home village. Truth to tell, he'd always had a roving eye, but he was a model family man now with a successful restaurant business in Rome. He'd begged his sons and daughters to visit him in Rome, but his departure from Yorkshire had left a legacy of bitterness and despair for Sandra Balboni.

In the same year he left, Olivia had miscarried her first pregnancy and slid into depression. It had thus been left to Julie to support her mother, sister and younger twin brothers. Carlo had visited Hemsdale some years earlier, but apart from Julie, no-one would see or speak to him. Now it occurred to her that it was high time the bitterness was put behind them.

'How about a trip to Italy to get to know your Italian relatives?' she asked Tim impulsively as he pulled on his dressing-gown.

'Yeah, maybe sometime. Right now I'd rather go to the cottage. Dad's coming over next month, isn't he?'

Julie smiled. 'Early summer holidays, that's what he promised us.'

'Great. I like it when it's just the three of us together, don't you? It's fun at the cottage. Can you and I go and get things ready one weekend?'

'I don't see why not.'

'Thanks, Mum, you're ace.' He planted a kiss on her cheek and headed for the bathroom.

Julie followed with the usual feeling of regret over what Tim had lost by his parents' divorce, however amicable the final separation had been after so much heartache in the short marriage.

It was a short drive from home to Tim's school, and conveniently in the same direction as Maldon's Pharmaceutical. As Tim ran to join his friends in the playground he called back to Julie.

'Mum, football practice tonight. Don't forget.'

'I won't. I'll pick you up, or Granny will. Five o'clock-ish . . . ' But Tim was already in the centre of a chattering group of friends.

Tim's school was in the centre of Hemsdale, a small market town in the Yorkshire Dales, surrounded by farmland and rolling landscapes of sheep-dotted hills. It was a lovely early summer morning and Julie wound down her window to breathe the clear country air as she left the town behind. She enjoyed the scenic trip to work, passing through hamlets with mellow stone cottages, and touching the fringes of the North Yorkshire Moors.

Maldon's Pharmaceutical was off the

beaten track, well concealed behind high stone walls, the main buildings discreetly low-built with reinforced thick glass windows which could be instantly shuttered if alarms were triggered. What animal research there had been in the past had long been abandoned, but the firm had a high profile in successful drug research and Managing Director Eric Lancaster was taking no chances.

Julie went straight to her boss's office on the first floor.

'Sorry I'm a bit late — the usual traffic on the school run.'

He nodded sympathetically. 'I'm glad to be done with all that — though I can see me as Grandad-on-duty there in the near future. Take a seat, Julie. Are you happy here?'

'Yes, I am. It was a good move.'

'So perhaps it's a good time to move on, develop other skills, take more responsibility?'

Julie's face displayed eager interest and anticipation as Eric continued.

'Our science boffins have come up with a drug which may possibly — only possibly — halt premature labour.'

'Goodness!' Julie leaned forward, excited.

'Indeed. But it's early days yet. I'm glad you've settled in so well here because I'd like you to organise the clinical trials.'

'Me?' she gasped. 'Surely that's a project manager's job?'

'Precisely. That's what I envisaged when we poached you from St Clements. I'm sure you know the procedures. I'll set up a board meeting, you write a research protocol by, say, Friday, present it to the board, they'll all agree and off you'll go.'

'Goodness!' Julie repeated, feeling excitement rise in her. She hadn't anticipated such a step-up quite so soon.

'Increase in salary, company car — you'll be doing a lot of mileage recruiting medical teams — hospitality budget. Maud will do you a new contract.' He reached for his jacket. 'I'm afraid I'll have to love you and leave you now — I'm due back at the conference. Oh, and, Julie, I suggest you start with recruiting at St Clements — it's always good to liase with the local hospital. Maud has the file. Good luck — Friday afternoon, don't forget.'

'Of course and . . . thank you.'

'Don't thank me, just do a good job. I know you will.'

Buoyed up by the challenge, Julie spent the rest of the morning reading up on her new project. It sounded interesting, and it was in her special area of interest. Her task wasn't to question the science, but to develop a management strategy for the research.

For reasons she couldn't fathom, she was reluctant to contact St Clements but obediently she made its maternity department her first recruitment call.

'Hi, Julie,' the receptionist said, recognising her name, 'I'm putting you through to maternity.'

Julie pictured the familiar scene on

the wards where she'd spent many happy years and suddenly felt nostalgic for its bustle and drama, and for the satisfying sense of joy when mothers gave birth.

'Julie, sorry to keep you.' The receptionist came back to her. 'No-one's free right now. Dan's in theatre, the new consultant's in a meeting, but Polly's just come in. Do you want to speak to her?'

Julie frowned. Dr Polly Fellowes was a prickly character, and apparently even more difficult since she'd been passed over for the plum job of senior consultant.

'All right, perhaps I'd better,' she replied.

'Julie, what's your problem?' Polly Fellowes barked, brusque and sharp, cross and in a hurry. 'It's a mad house here and you're well out of it with your cushy number. What do you want?'

'It's about clinical trials I'm organising — a new drug . . . '

'Gracious — you're organising?

Rapid promotion, eh?'

'Er . . . I suppose so, but . . . '

'Can't help . . . no time,' Polly broke in abruptly. 'Ask the new boss.'

'Um . . . all right. When's he starting?

'Days ago, but he's not here yet . . . Yes?' She broke off and Julie heard her talking to someone else: 'How should I know? Tell him . . . Wait, *I'll* tell him. Sorry, Julie, got to dash.'

Julie hung up, quite relieved that St Clements was obviously out of the picture and she didn't have to deal with Polly again.

Her phone rang again almost immediately. It was Olivia, breathless and excited.

'Julie, can you make it to supper tonight? Michael's flying home straight away — he'll get in this afternoon. He'll want to talk to you. Oh, and that friend of yours, the senior registrar. Dick, is it?'

'Dan,' Julie corrected.

'Dan then — bring him. I need to know someone on the inside. It's a pity

you left, you could have helped deliver
. . . I'm so excited.'

'That's great — but I can't come
tonight. I promised Tim . . . '

'I've an appointment at the hospital
tomorrow,' Olivia broke in. 'I want you
to brief me.'

'What for? You've been pregnant
before.'

'That was years ago! I expect it's all
different now. Can you make it
tomorrow then, after my hospital visit?'

'Olivia, I have work to do . . . '

'You can spare me a couple of hours,
surely?' Olivia persisted. 'You needn't
stay late. Please?'

'I'll see how things go. I'm not
promising, and of course, I can't speak
for Dan.'

'Perfect.' As usual Olivia swept aside
all objections. 'Seven o'clock. I'll get
Ellena to cook something special. Bye!'

With resigned exasperation Julie
sighed and phoned Dan on his mobile,
intending to leave a message. She
was surprised when he answered

immediately. Hadn't Polly said he was in theatre?

'Sure, love to,' he replied when she told him of the invitation. 'I could do with a slice of social life away from the hospital. Your sister lives in Pendale Court, doesn't she? I'll be interested to see how the really rich people live! I'll pick you up.

'The new man starts tomorrow, by the way. We had a meeting today. He's a great guy — a real live-wire. Hey, don't forget bowling on Saturday. We — oh, that's my pager, must rush.'

Busy, busy world, Julie thought guiltily as she sat in the calm of her office surrounded by beautiful tranquil countryside. She began to work her way through her list of possible recruits for clinical trials of the proposed new drug.

An hour or so later her enthusiasm was considerably dampened by the responses. From consultants to mid-wives they were lukewarm: 'Sorry, not my area of interest.' 'Too busy coping with the birthrate here.' 'Not worth the risk.' By the end of the day she began to think her managing director had handed her a poisoned chalice.

Conscious of her promise to Tim, she left early, taking the new file home, but Tim had been invited to an impromptu sleepover so she was free to work through the evening.

Just as her eyes were beginning to glaze over with costs and projections her mother knocked at the door of the flat.

'What's this?' Julie laughed as she opened the door and found a bottle of wine being waved before her.

'We're celebrating your promotion, dear.'

'I thought we did that last night.'

'This is just for you and me. It's a rare occasion for the house to be so quiet.'

'Lovely. I'll open the posh biscuits Geoff sent over from America at Christmas.'

'How is he?'

'Fine, as far as I know. He'll be

visiting over the summer holidays — we'll all go to the cottage.'

Sandra poured wine into glasses, handed one to Julie and raised her own. 'Here's to us.'

'To us,' Julie echoed, 'and my everlasting thanks for all you do for us, Tim and me.'

'It's a pleasure. He's a lovely boy, very well balanced considering . . . '

'Yes, we're lucky. And he's got you and Ed and Sam.'

Sandra sipped her wine, looked at her attractive daughter and took the plunge. 'You know, you . . . you . . . '

'No, Mum.' Julie anticipated what would come next. 'I'm not thinking of getting married again. I haven't time, Mum, and I made such a mess of it last time I'd be scared. I'm happy, and so lucky with my family here.

'I'm going to supper with Olivia tomorrow. Michael's home and I'm ordered to take Dan to provide inside information on St Clements maternity department.'

'Your sister takes a lot for granted and a lot of your time. She should stand on her own feet more . . . '

'I don't mind,' Julie interrupted. 'I feel sort of responsible for her.'

Sandra frowned. 'I know you do, and I know why, but she has a husband, lots of money . . . '

'She's desperate for a baby.'

'Well,' Sandra pressed her lips together then shrugged. 'Sorry, touchy subject. So, tell me about this grand new job you've got.'

'It's going to be very interesting . . . ' Julie began, relieved to be on safer ground.

★ ★ ★

'Wow,' Dan watched the electronic gates of Pendale Court swing open. 'What does this Michael do for a living?'

'Debentures or something. He moves money about. I'm not sure . . . '

The evening was a success. Olivia was radiant and Michael was full of paternal pride already. He opened champagne.

'A toast — to our baby.'

Olivia sipped water. 'Pray and hope,' she said.

'Congratulations,' Dan said. 'Do you know which hospital you'll be going to to have the baby?'

'St Clements.' Olivia was firm.

Her husband looked astonished. 'But . . .'

'St Clements,' repeated Olivia, 'and I'll tell you why. I have absolutely no worries now about our baby. And I met the new consultant today. He's a wonder — a local boy.'

Julie's heart lurched. 'What's his name?'

But she knew the answer, of course — had done ever since she'd glimpsed that figure at the back of the hall.

'Robert Kendall. He's going to monitor my pregnancy personally.'

Julie took a gulp of champagne. Robert Kendall — returned from the past to revive all her adolescent misery and insecurities; come to remind her of that long-buried gawky fifteen-year-old with braces on her teeth and an aching crush on the most popular head boy at Fletcher Comprehensive. *That* Robert Kendall!

Olivia was prattling on about the new consultant but Julie hardly heard until her sister pulled her attention back to the present.

'He must be around your age. Do you remember him?'

'Oh . . . um . . . maybe . . . This goulash of Ellena's is great. Would she give me the recipe?'

'Sure, but you must come with me for my next appointment — you can meet Robert Kendall.'

'I don't think so, I'm really pushed at work . . . ' Julie hedged.

Fortunately Michael's mobile rang, for the fourth time since supper had started, which created a distraction, and after the call he gave them a run-down on the current state of financial opportunities in Dubai which fascinated Dan.

Finally Dan and Julie pleaded work pressures and left early, with Olivia's entreaties to come again ringing in their ears.

'I enjoyed that,' Dan said. 'Thanks for asking me. Your sister's quite a lot older than you, isn't she?'

'Ten years. She's thirty-nine, so I hope her pregnancy's OK.'

'I've no doubt it will be with the dynamic Mr Kendall in charge. What was he like at school?'

'Popular, good-looking, bright, football captain, head boy . . . '

'I thought you said you hardly knew him!'

'It was difficult not to know *of* him though.'

'He'll make waves at St Clements. Even Polly . . . '

'Do we have to talk about him?' she broke in. 'I'm disliking him already, the way everyone's going on about him,' she said crossly.

'Fine by me. How about bowling

with Tim? Would Wednesday suit you?'

'The weekend would be best. How about Saturday? We'll pick you up. Thanks for coming tonight, Dan.'

'Pleasure.' He drew up outside her house. 'See you Saturday, then. Goodnight, Julie.'

★　★　★

On Thursday evening, Julie went to see Eric Lancaster to plead for an extension on the drug trial.

'You're in luck.' He beamed. 'I've had to postpone until Monday anyway. Having trouble?'

'No, it just needs a tweak here and there. It's been hard work persuading the medics that this drug will help their careers along, but I'm nearly there.'

'I've got good news for you then. I met St Clements' new senior consultant yesterday and he's really interested — very happy to be involved. I told him you're project manager. Apparently he went to the local comprehensive, maybe around your time. Do you know him? Robert Kendall?'

'Oh yes,' she said, 'I've heard of him. He's several years older than me.'

'Ah, that's why your name didn't ring a bell with him. But he'll be in touch. He thought a new drug like ours could help his work abroad.'

'I did get in touch with St Clements but they weren't interested.'

He shrugged. 'New broom, new ideas. You'll like him.'

She felt a hollow feeling in the pit of her stomach.

* * *

By Saturday afternoon Julie knew she'd be hard put to finish her management strategy plan for the drug trial by Monday, especially as Sunday was family roast dinner time and her mother had had a migraine since Friday. She was still in bed when Julie went to check on her.

'I'll be fine, dear. You know how these

things run. I'll be as right as rain in the morning. It always happens when there's a storm brewing. It'll break tonight and then I'll feel better.'

'I was taking Tim bowling with Dan but I could cancel . . . '

'Don't cancel; go and enjoy yourselves. Please.'

'OK, but I'll go a bit later.'

Julie called Dan. 'Mum's got a migraine and I still have a bit of work to do.'

'OK. I've already booked the rink for seven, so I'll pick up Tim and you can follow when you can. We're better bowlers than you anyway.'

'Cheek! But if you're sure. Tim's getting restless here and Mum needs a new prescription, so I've got to . . . '

'Stop flapping, Julie. It's OK. I'll be round in half an hour.'

'Take your waterproofs, there's a storm brewing and . . . '

'Julie! It's an indoor rink. Stop fussing. What's the matter with you?'

'Oh, I'm just a bit harassed. I don't

know . . . I'm fine. See you.'

Once she'd waved Tim and Dan off, the house was quiet. She whipped through the final draft of her protocol on her laptop and printed it out just as the first rumbles of thunder growled in the sky and raindrops spattered on the windows.

She checked her mother, who was now sound asleep, before she left. The rain was coming down in such a deluge that she switched the wipers to fast and decreased her speed, pulling in to the side of the road once or twice as visibility reduced to almost zero. Lightning flashed as thunder cracked the sky but after a last monstrous rattle the storm began to ease, the rain reducing to a steady downpour accompanied by sulky rumbles growing ever more distant as the summer storm moved on.

She breathed a sigh of relief and drove on to the sports centre.

The bowling alleys were all full and she couldn't see either Dan or Tim. She went to the cafeteria, but they weren't there. Back in the bowling alleys, there was still no sign. A frisson of alarm went through her. They should still be here; they couldn't have gone out into the storm, and she'd rung Dan's mobile before she left and they were bowling then. She rang him again.

'Dan, where are you?'

'Julie — thank goodness! I can't find Tim!'

'You've lost Tim?' Her voice cracked with anxiety. 'What . . . ?'

'He can't be far away. I'm in the office now and they're about to page him on the Tannoy. He's probably met a mate somewhere.'

'Tim's not like that. Why did you let him go . . . ?'

'I didn't. He said he was going to the shop to get a drink.'

The Tannoy crackled and a voice boomed out: 'Tim Haywood — will Tim Haywood come to Reception, please? Tim Haywood . . . ' The message was played three times.

'Is he there?' Julie pleaded.

'Not yet, give him time. Don't worry,' but Dan's own voice was sharp with anxiety.

'Don't worry? Dan, he's only ten years old.'

'But he's a sensible ten. Look, if he's not here, they'll try again in a few minutes.'

'I'm coming to meet you. I'll ask at the shop on my way.'

At the shop the girl remembered Tim. 'Good looking little boy, very polite, not like some we get in here. He asked for a Super Smoothie but we don't have them, so I told him to ask at the supermarket.'

'Did he go outside the centre?'

The girl frowned. 'I'm not sure. There was a queue behind him and I'm on my own. Is he lost?'

'I hope not.'

Julie clutched Dan's arm as he came running to meet her. 'He's gone out, to the supermarket probably. Dan, he's been gone over half an hour.'

'We'll find him.' He turned to the girl

at the counter, 'Can you watch out for him and if he comes back tell him to wait?'

'Don't worry,' the girl said. 'I'll keep him by me and I'll tell Security to check — and I'll watch the door.'

'The supermarket's this way,' Julie said, running toward the town centre. The roads were streaming wet, it was still cloudy and a thick misty drizzle cloaked the street. There was no sign of anyone on the streets. The shopping parade was several hundred yards away.

'What were you thinking of, letting him go ..?' she panted. 'And he's scared of thunder.'

'I'm sorry . . . '

'There he is!' Julie suddenly shrieked. 'Tim!' She ran towards him, registering as she did that there was a man with him. He was standing in the shadows of the doorway but she could see that they were chatting animatedly.

'I'm not really scared of thunder,' Tim was saying. 'It's just the lightning.

Once, in America . . . Mum! What's up?'

'What's up?' Julie was almost crying with relief. She grabbed hold of him and glared at the stranger. 'What do you think you're doing with my son? I'll report . . .'

'No, Mum, it's OK,' Tim broke in.. 'I got caught in the rain and this man loaned me his rain jacket and stayed with me until it stopped.'

'For goodness' sake!' Julie shrieked. 'You know better than that.'

'He's not a stranger, Mum. He knows Granny.'

The man moved forward and held out his hand.

'I'm sorry you were worried. Tim was caught in that downpour. I just took him into the shop then waited with him for the storm to stop and here we are. I work at St Clements. Hi, it's Dan, isn't it? You work there too, don't you? We've met — Robert Kendall.'

'Mr Kendall?' Dan peered into the darkness. 'Of course, it's so dark tonight, I didn't recognise you. Thanks for looking after Tim. I'm in the dog-house with his mum here.'

'No, no, it's fine now, Dan, now that we've found him. Thanks . . . er, Mr Kendall, but we must go. I'll get Tim home.'

'Mum, we haven't finished bowling yet.'

'It's late and Granny's not well. Come on. Thanks again.' Julie bent her head as Robert Kendall offered her his hand to shake. Briefly she touched it and jumped as though it was a burning coal.

He peered at her, nodded politely and turned away.

'Bye, Tim. See you, Dan. Mrs . . . er . . . '

But Julie had already turned away. Although there hadn't been the slightest flicker of recognition on his face, she'd have known him anywhere.

Meeting Robert Kendall

The Balbonis often met for Sunday lunch at Loughrigg, the family home. Traditionally the last Sunday of each month was kept free by all if possible, to allow them to meet and catch up on family news. The tradition was precious to Sandra Balboni, so she was pleased that her migraine had eased after Saturday night's storm.

This particular Sunday was a beautiful day, bright and sunny, the grey skies washed to a pure blue by the heavy showers. Sandra was up and about but still feeling fragile so Julie was in charge for lunch and glad to be busy enough to put the previous night's encounter with Robert Kendall to the back of her mind.

Sam was the first to phone. 'Julie, hi. I've got news.' His voice was taut with excitement and Julie could hear Jane's laughter in the background.

'Good news, I hope.'

'Yes. Jane and I are getting married.'

'Wow! That's great. It's about time. Mum'll be ecstatic, she loves Jane — we all do. Congratulations.'

'Thanks. How about dusting off the barbecue gear and having a celebratory lunch in the garden? We'll bring stuff over.'

'No need, there's plenty here. Mum did a massive shop before her migraine struck. I'll make a fruit punch and there are piles of sausages and steaks in the freezer.'

'We'll bring some things anyway. Are Olivia and Mike coming?'

'I think so — last Sunday in the month is a sort of royal command.'

'Good. It's a double celebration then: Jane and me, and a new baby.'

'Lovely. Come early, Tim'll love to help set up the barbecue.'

'OK. I'll phone Eddie. Who's his latest girlfriend?'

'Sally, I think. The girl from local

radio. And I'll phone Olivia. Have you set a date for the wedding?'

'Soon, we hope. There's no point in hanging about, is there?'

'None at all. Er . . . do you think you'll be inviting Dad?'

'I haven't thought about it. Depends on Mum.' Sam was non-committal. 'We'll talk about it some other time. I don't want anything to upset today. See you later.'

With a sigh, Julie hung up. The twins' bitterness still ran deep, which was sad. Julie had come to realise that her parents, stolidly English Sandra and volatile Italian Carlo, had been mis-matched from the start although their early years together had apparently been very happy. Olivia was named after Carlo's mother and Julie remem-bered childhood summer holidays spent at the Balbonis' villa in the Umbrian hills.

Carlo had hated the cold British winters and was always planning to escape to Italy to open a restaurant with his English family. Sandra had resisted the move, however. Hemsdale was her home and her family tree had long roots.

Carlo had persisted in looking for his ideal restaurant location and eventually found it near his native village. Unfortunately he had also found young Italian Isabella and fallen in love with her. His Hemsdale family had never forgiven him — at least, none apart from Julie.

Standing in the hall, Julie's thoughts drifted on to Marietta, an Italian lady from Rome who had gone into premature labour while touring England with her family a year or so ago. Julie had been the midwife on duty who had delivered Marietta's baby boy.

Amazingly, Marietta had known Carlo and his new family and had told Julie of his life in Rome.

'We know him well and we often dine at his wonderful restaurant. He has two lovely children but he talks sadly of his English family who will not see or speak to him.'

'But he left us!' Julie had protested. 'My mother was ill for ages; my sister miscarried her first baby and hasn't been able to conceive since.'

Marietta cradled her beautiful baby, her eyes dreamy.

'This baby, Paulo, is our third child, a gift we treasure in our family.' She shrugged. 'Carlo Balboni has given you a wonderful gift, he has extended the family boundaries. There are now more to love. Isn't that worth forgiveness?'

'I doubt if my mother would ever see it like that,' Julie had said, but Marietta's words had stayed with her, especially when her own divorce had deprived Tim of his father. Since her divorce, she had sent Christmas cards to the Italian Balbonis and Carlo had responded eagerly, anxious for reconciliation and forgiveness. So far, Sandra was adamant that she had no wish to be reminded of the draining years of depression following Carlo's departure.

Julie snapped her mind back to the

present. Perhaps Sam's wedding would be an opportunity to try again. She knew Jane was intrigued by the Italian connection and was anxious to meet Sam's father. She sighed. Only time would tell.

The weather held, the sun growing warmer by the hour. Sam and Jane glowed with happiness as the family toasted their future together. Olivia and Michael were quietly content, and Eddie turned up in the company of a beautiful girl called Vanda.

'So much for Sally,' Jane murmured to Julie. 'Where does he find them all?'

'She's lovely though, and Tim's really taken with her.'

'For twin brothers, Eddie and Sam are so different.' Jane's eyes were full of love as she watched her fiancé, busy with the barbecue.

Sandra sat in the shade, happy and proud of her family. Julie took her a dish of salad.

'You look so much better, Mum. Isn't

this lovely, a family gathering?'

'I hope you caught it on camera, dear, it's what families are all about.'

'I'm sure Michael has — he has a new camcorder.'

'That's good. When's Geoff coming over?'

Julie stifled a sigh. She knew what was coming next.

'Probably Spring Bank Holiday for a few days, then again in the summer. He's taking a longer break for Tim's summer holiday this year.'

'That's wonderful. If only . . . '

'No! We're friends, Ma, but there's no hope of us getting back together — you must accept that.'

'I know, but you seem to get on so well together. When he was over in the new year . . . '

'Mum! That's because we're *not* married now. I like Geoff, and for Tim's sake we'll always stay friends. But that's all.'

The two women fell silent. The late afternoon sun gilded the garden. Eddie had organised a cricket game and shouts and laughter filled the air.

'Mum,' Julie began tentatively, 'about Sam's wedding. Don't you think . . . maybe Dad and . . . his family . . . It'd be nice to meet his . . . '

'I don't think so, Julie, and I'm surprised you should think of it.'

'But if Sam and Jane . . . ?'

'That's their business but I'll tell you one thing — if he's there, then I won't be.' She smiled sadly. 'I know you think I'm a hard woman but . . . I can't. I'm not ready — I don't know if I ever will be.'

'Of course. I'm sorry too. It's none of my business.'

'But it is, and if you want to visit your father and his family in Italy I shan't mind. Truly. Tim should meet his Italian relatives, broaden his outlook. I don't believe he should spend the whole of his life in Hemsdale.' Very softly, so that Julie could hardly hear her, she added, 'I think that was my big mistake.'

Julie was surprised. Yet perhaps it might just be a crack in the door . . .

*   *   *

On Monday morning, Julie settled back into her work routine. She still had work to do from her S.A.D. protocol. Lots of e-mails had come in over the weekend. The board was considering her drug trial presentation and at any moment she expected to be sent for by them.

There was no summons, however, and just before lunchtime, Eric Lancaster came into her office and slapped a file on her desk.

'Well done, Julie — passed without a quibble. They even voted you an increase in the hospitality budget so that you can steam ahead. I'd advise you to contact the local guy first — Robert Kendall at St Clements. Fix a meeting.'

'I'm a bit snowed under just now, finishing off the S.A.D. work . . .'

'Teresa will take care of any loose ends — she needs the experience and we're keen to get going on the new project. So go ahead with fixing up the clinical trials. Shall I contact Robert Kendall?'

'No, no, I'll do that.'

'Good-oh. Good weekend?'

'Yes, very. On Sunday we had a family gathering, and we have a future wedding and a pregnancy — separate couples!' she added.

He grinned. 'I can't wait for my grandsons to grow up a bit so that I can teach them cricket, fishing, golf . . . ' He walked off, still mentally listing future events to share with his grandchildren.

Julie couldn't help feeling she was living in some sort of commercial for happy families, and with Geoff's visit looming, she'd be in the thick of it too. She knew Tim badly missed his dad, but Geoff took every opportunity to visit him.

Forcing her mind back to work, she

contacted St Clements. Robert Kendall was unavailable so she left a message and went to find Teresa.

She phoned again first thing next morning and couldn't help feeling relieved to hear that Robert Kendall was away for a couple of days. It was ridiculous but she couldn't rid herself of those devastating feelings from her teenage years — the humiliation of rejection.

She threw herself into lining up her other contacts who would be taking part in the clinical trials for the new drug, and was visiting another hospital when Robert Kendall finally left a message with a precise instruction to ring his office between two and three o'clock the next day.

Pleased with the contacts already confirmed, Julie did so, ignoring the nervous flutter in her stomach.

'Julie Haywood here, Mr Kendall's expecting my call,' she said, with a lot more confidence than she felt.

The receptionist knew her. 'Julie! Hello.

How are you? We still miss you here.'

'That's nice of you, but I'll probably be around St Clements quite a lot in the future — I'll be working with Mr Kendall.'

'Lucky you. He's lovely. We've all fallen for him! I'm connecting you now.'

'Rob Kendall here.' His voice sounded brisk and businesslike.

'Hi. Julie Haywood, Maldon's Pharmaceutical. My managing director, Eric Lancaster . . .'

'Yes, I remember.' He sounded distant and preoccupied.

'Mr Lancaster said you were interested in undertaking our latest clinical trials. I'd like to set up a meeting soon.'

'A meeting? What for? Can't you just go ahead? Though to be honest, I'm beginning to think I was rather foolish to volunteer. I hadn't actually started the job here then, you see,' he explained. 'My fault, of course, but I'd forgotten the pressure here. There was pressure in Africa but it was very different from here — more hands-on, less paperwork. Still, that's another story. Sorry, Mrs . . . um . . . Haywood?'

'Julie, please.'

'OK, Julie, let's meet at the hospital, say tomorrow midday-ish. I'll see what it'll involve.'

'I'd be grateful for your time,' Julie agreed quickly. 'Can I buy you lunch? The Four Feathers is just round the corner from St Clements.'

'I don't usually have the luxury of a lunch-hour worthy of the Feathers. What's wrong with the hospital canteen? I've seen worse.'

'I used to work at St Clements, in Maternity,' Julie explained. 'There would be too many distractions, too many people wanting to chat.'

'Fair enough. The Feathers it is then. One o'clock. I'll see you then.'

⋆ ⋆ ⋆

Next morning, after taking Tim to school, Julie worked from home.

Paperwork and phone calls occupied her until noon but the meeting with Robert Kendall loomed too large for concentration. As the clock struck twelve she snapped shut her laptop and opened her wardrobe. The Feathers had a smart restaurant and bistro, and she'd booked a table in the restaurant which was often used for business meetings and deals. She pulled out her best black suit, her conference suit; there had to be no trace of that awkward schoolgirl.

As she left the house her mother drove into the drive.

'Goodness Julie, you look smart. Is it a meeting? A conference?'

'A business meeting.' She took her mother's shopping and carried it back into the house for her.

'I'm not sure about the hair,' Sandra observed. 'You don't usually scrape it back like that. It's a bit severe, it doesn't suit you.'

Julie bent to kiss her. 'It's just an experiment, sort of a disguise. Must dash! See you later.'

★ ★ ★

In fact she was ten minutes early. She'd booked a table in the restaurant but waited in the bar.

On the dot of one o'clock Robert Kendall came into the bar and she pressed her hand to her chest to still her thumping heart.

She remembered him as a tall slim schoolboy, nearly nineteen, with a mop of dark hair. Over the years, he had filled out, was more muscular, and his hair was shorter. Now he was a very attractive man, though there were still traces of the boy she had dreamed about every night of his last summer term at Fletcher Comprehensive.

She swallowed hard. He was older now and so was she — well beyond such foolishness.

He was looking round the bar and his eyes swept past Julie without a hint of recognition. She stepped forward.

'Robert Kendall. I'm Julie — pleased

to meet you. I've booked a table in the restaurant.'

'Can't we just grab a sandwich here? I don't feel I could do the restaurant justice. I'm operating this afternoon.'

'Of course,' she said. 'I'll cancel the reservation.'

She handed him a bar menu and for the first time he looked directly at her, taking in the smart suit, dark glasses and severe hairstyle. His eyebrows raised a fraction and she turned away in panic.

'Er — Mrs Haywood . . . Julie?' He was looking at her intently. 'I've seen you somewhere before — recently,' he said. 'I haven't been back long so it must be recent.'

'I don't think so,' she said, opening her briefcase and pulling out a wad of papers. 'These are my plans for the trials . . . '

He frowned. 'If it's already done, why the meeting?'

'Well . . . um . . . Eric likes me to establish personal contact. We might hate each other,' she floundered. 'What I mean is, we need a certain measure of compatibility, don't you agree?'

He leaned back, an amused grin twitching his mouth.

'Well, Julie, I guess we could rub along *if* I agree to do the trials. It could be useful in Ghana if I go back there.'

'Do you plan to go back?'

'I haven't any long-term plan as yet, but I should think I'll be at St Clements for a while.' He picked up the papers, glancing through them.

'These are only suggestions,' she said quickly. 'It's only because I know St Clements so well that I was able to make a provisional plan. Feel free to reject or pick bits out of it.'

'I will. I'll ring you. Perhaps tomorrow.' His pager trilled and he glanced at it. 'Sorry, I have to leave,' he said.

'But you'll take the trials?'

'Maybe. I'll be in touch. Do you have a personal interest in this?'

'Not really, though my sister had a

premature labour ten years ago. The baby died.'

'I'm sorry.' He was staring intently at her again. 'There's no sun in here, so why the dark glasses?'

'Er . . . an eye infection,' she fibbed.

'Let me look.' Before she could stop him, he gently removed her glasses. 'Aha, as I thought! The memory's been teasing my brain since I came in here. You're the girl on the conference platform — last week's conference on S.A.D. I was held up and just heard the last minute or two. You seemed to have captured your audience.' He looked at her more closely. 'But there's something else . . . way back . . . '

Julie sighed. 'I'm Julie Balboni. Haywood's my married name. We were both at Fletcher Comprehensive — you were in the sixth form, I was third year.'

'Were you? So Olivia's your sister — I saw her last week as a patient. And through her I see your interest in this drug trial.' He stood up just as the barman brought over their sandwiches.

'Sorry, I have to go.' He scooped up the papers and his jacket. 'Do you know, when I was in the third form, all the lads were madly in love with Olivia. She was a stunner. I once came to your house with some other boys just for a glimpse of her. Your mother was really kind to us — she let us down lightly. And I can see a resemblance. You have the same eyes as Olivia — eloquent and expressive. But sorry, Julie, I don't remember you at all.'

Thank goodness for that, Julie thought

An Unexpected Visit

A brief e-mail the following morning informed Julie that Rob was prepared to set up clinical trials at St Clements. He agreed Julie's strategy with a few minor changes. Perhaps he would involve a colleague to ease the workload. Details would be finalised by telephone.

Julie felt an irrational disappointment that she wouldn't be seeing Rob in person. Yet she could never forget that cruel snub of years ago. He might not remember but she would never forget it.

She scrolled through the rest of her e-mails. To her surprise the name on the last of them was Carlo Balboni! Her father usually e-mailed her every six months or so and she always enjoyed the newsy gossip about his children, his restaurant, and the pleasures of his beloved Italy. This time she'd heard from him only a month earlier.

As always, the e-mail ended, *One day I hope to share these pleasures with ALL my children. I look forward to that time, dear Julie. From your loving father, Carlo Balboni.*

'Maybe sooner than you think,' Julie mused, thinking how good it would be to take Tim to meet his Italian relatives. Now she had her mother's tacit agreement, she could take advantage of her father's offer.

It was to be a morning of interruptions. Between all her work calls, Olivia rang and Julie's heart sank. Since her pregnancy, her sister had taken to phoning in a daily account of her condition.

'Touch of morning sickness this morning,' Olivia announced proudly. 'Now it really feels as though I'm pregnant. Isn't that good?'

'If you think so, yes. Olivia, can I ring you tonight? I'm snowed under just now.'

'Oh, all right. I'll phone Mum. Wasn't that a lovely party on Sunday? Vanda was . . .'

'Please, Olivia, let's chat tonight. I've a mountain of stuff to do. I'll ring you.' Julie felt disapproval in the frosty silence. 'Sorry,' she added.

'Oh well, if you're too busy . . . just one thing quickly: you know Rob Kendall? I'm going to ask him to supper one night. Will you come too?'

'Not such a good idea.'

'Whyever not?'

'It's unprofessional. It could put him in a difficult position.'

'Oh, rubbish. He's so charming, and an old school friend, for goodness' sake. And you should be thinking of finding someone . . . It's time you had a man again, a father for Tim . . .'

'Tim's got a father.'

'You know what I mean. Anyway Rob Kendall being my obstetrician has nothing to do with it. He knows Michael from schooldays and he's asking his financial advice. Apparently he's inherited some money from a great aunt.'

'Bully for him. Anyway I'm going to the cottage this weekend with Tim, to get ready for Geoff's visit. I must go, I'll talk to you tonight.'

An added benefit of Julie's promotion was a shared secretary, whom she now called. 'Lucy, could you hold all my calls for an hour? Unless you think there's an urgent one, of course.'

'That's a coincidence,' Lucy replied. 'Mr Kendall from St Clements is on the line. Will you speak to him?'

'Sure, put him through.'

'Julie? How are you?' he asked.

'Fine. I got your e-mail and I'm very pleased you've decided to do the trials.'

'Yes, well, your plan seems very efficient. But I should just confirm one thing. I've a colleague who's expressed an interest in helping. Polly Fellowes. She heard about it and . . . '

'Polly?' Julie interrupted. 'But she didn't want anything to do with it when I asked her.'

'She's obviously changed her mind. She'll be useful, I think. She's a hard worker, if perhaps a bit . . . er . . . '

'Abrasive?' Julie supplied.

He laughed. 'You said it, not me.' There was silence and Julie was about to ask if there was anything else when he said, 'I'm sorry I had to cut lunch short the other say. Perhaps another time?'

Julie was nonplussed. Was he asking her out, or was it to discuss the trials further? She decided to avoid the issue.

'I expect we'll be in touch. If you let me know your starting date, I'll arrange to meet with you. And Polly,' she added as an afterthought.

'We'll look forward to that. I find the cafeteria here does an excellent cheese sandwich.'

He rang off, leaving her to puzzle over the inclusion of Polly Fellowes. Polly was notorious for avoiding things not directly concerning her own patient care. She was a good doctor but had little time for what she called 'the fripperies' of medicine, clinical trials being, in her book, a frippery. Maybe, Julie thought, she had fallen for the charms of Robert Kendall.

As she turned back to her laptop, a message popped up on the screen: *Arriving earlier than planned, business conference in York. Will keep you informed. Alert Tim. Love to all, Geoff.*

After work she picked Tim up from school and showed him both Carlo's and his father's e-mails.

'Great. We must get the cottage ready for Dad this weekend. Can we, Mum, please?'

'Sure, isn't that what we planned anyway? Tell you what, I'll wangle Friday afternoon off and we can go straight from school. How's that?'

'Cool! Do you think he'll be here at the weekend?'

'I don't know, he'll let us know. Now, how about Grandpa Carlo's offer?'

Tim looked doubtful. 'I'll be at school. After this half term, I don't break up until July.'

'July would be fine — or we could do a weekend. A weekend might be best, actually. We could see the sights, meet Grandpa . . . '

'Wouldn't Granny mind?' Tim asked. 'She won't go, will she?'

'No, but she doesn't mind if we go. She told me so. In fact she thinks it would be good for you to see a bit of the world outside Hemsdale.'

'I've been to London . . . and Scotland,' he protested. 'And the States. We lived there, didn't we?'

'Of course, but you can't remember much about that surely? You were only just over four when we left.'

'I do! I liked it there — and I liked Dad being there too.'

'Oh, Tim.' She gave him a hug. 'I'm sorry, love, it was . . . '

'It's OK, I'm fine. Don't worry — Dad's coming over soon and I'll like it then.' He wriggled out of her grasp. 'I'm fine, Mum, honest. Love you,' he muttered as he ran into the house. She heard him calling out to Sandra, 'I'm home, Gran, got any flapjacks today?'

Julie followed more slowly. Tim was growing up fast. On the surface, he'd survived the divorce well. Many of his friends had divorced parents too, and children were survivors. Perhaps she and Geoff should have worked harder to keep the marriage going, though?

She followed him into the house. Tea and flapjacks sounded very comforting.

*   *   *

Tim helped Julie load her roomy estate car with provisions for the cottage she and Geoff co-owned, number 2 Moorland View. Built of local mellowed stone, it nestled near the foot of a hillside which climbed up to the moors where sheep grazed in summer and huddled against the stone sheds in winter. The cottage front looked down on the village of Tanby, once a small hamlet of farm workers, now a mecca for fell and moorland walkers. It had been Julie and Geoff's first marital home.

A ruin when they'd bought it, they'd done it up with love and care in the early happy days of their marriage. During the divorce there had never been a question of selling it. It was her bolthole and a home for Geoff during his increasingly frequent visits from America.

As she and Tim drove out of Hemsdale, their spirits lifted. The weather was kind and Tim was looking forward to his half term holiday at the cottage. She had her laptop and files and could easily travel to and from the office once Geoff arrived during the week.

'I see it!' Tim pointed. 'Look, there's smoke coming from the chimney. Uncle Harry must have lit the fires.'

'I phoned him during the week. He and Alice will have given it an airing.'

Through the village and up the hill they drove, to the cottage, where their elderly neighbours, Henry and Alice

Lunn, were outside the gate, wide smiles on their faces. They were a courtesy aunt and uncle who were very fond of the young family and took a great interest in Tim.

'Lovely to see you again, dears.' Alice hugged first Julie then Tim who suffered the motherly smothering with good grace. A couple of collie crosses yapped and barked around them and chased away the hens that came clucking by to see what all the fuss was about.

Harry shook hands with Tim and kissed Julie. 'Great to see you — it's a sign that summer's coming. Is Geoff arriving soon?'

'We hope so, but we're not quite sure when. Oh, Harry, you've tidied the garden! How kind you are.'

'It was a pleasure, you know that.'

'He hasn't enough to do since he retired so he loves looking after your place like it's his own,' said Alice. 'We'll let you settle in now. I've left some home-made vegetable soup on the hob and there's a dozen eggs on the dresser, new-laid this morning.' She ruffled Tim's hair. 'Drop by and collect some more eggs when you've finished those.'

'I will, Auntie Alice. Thanks.'

The couple lived a little farther down from number 2, and not far from the small village. When Julie and Geoff first moved into their cottage, Harry had helped with the rebuilding and restoration and Alice had been a great support after Tim had been born. They'd been happy years — all too few — before Geoff was bitten by the American bug which strained their marriage to breaking point.

Tim ran in and out of the cottage, unpacking his things in his favourite room under the eaves. He loved the sweeping view from his window, the village laid out beneath him like a miniature toytown fringing the green hills behind it.

'Tim! Lunch!' Julie called from the kitchen and he bounded down the stairs.

'Mum, can we have a dog like Patch?'

'Patch is a working dog, not really suitable for Hemsdale.'

'No, I mean here.'

'But, Tim, we don't live here, and we're out all day in Hemsdale.'

'Granny would look after him.'

'Granny's got enough to do without a dog to look after.'

'When's Dad coming?' Tim picked at his bread and ignored his soup.

'You know I don't know that. He'll let us know soon enough. Finish your soup.'

He took a couple of mouthfuls then laid his spoon on the table.

'Mum, why did you and Dad split up?' he asked suddenly. 'Didn't you like our house in America?'

It was the first time Tim had asked her about the break-up. Up to now, he'd appeared to have accepted the situation. He had a sweet disposition, didn't like confrontations and seemed to relish his Hemsdale family.

'It was warm, we had a swimming

pool, I remember that,' he said. 'And I don't remember you and Dad ever fighting.'

'We didn't. We tried never to argue in front of you, but . . . '

'You were happy, there were parties. I *do* remember. I was only frightened once — in that hurricane when the lightning struck a . . . a sort of tractor.'

'That was a mower. But, Tim, you weren't even five years old.'

'But I do remember — and you haven't said why you split up.'

'I . . . I can't truthfully explain. When you're older . . . '

'Liam knows why his mum left — she found another man. Did you do that?'

'No, of course I didn't! I just . . . didn't like America, or the way of life. I missed home — Mum, Sam, Eddie . . . ' It was impossible for her to tell him about Lyndy.

He nodded. 'But you could have had visits back here.'

'Tim, you just have to trust me. When I think you're able to understand

more . . . adults are complicated, and
. . . relationships . . . '

He picked up his spoon and smiled.
'OK, we'll talk later.' He giggled. 'When
I'm older — eh? Can we go to the
market tomorrow morning?'

'Yes, of course. I know Gran's given
you some pocket money to spend.'

'Can we go down to the river this
afternoon? Dad'll want to go fishing so
I'll check out the rods and lines.
They're in the shed, aren't they?'

'They were the last time. I'll be ready
in a few minutes and we could go to
that DVD place to get a film to watch
tonight.'

'Uhuh, maybe.'

She watched him through the kitchen
window as he went round to the cluster
of outhouses that belonged to the
cottage, and it occurred to her suddenly
that the set of his shoulders was
different — more embryonic man than
young boy. He was no longer a little
boy, he was nearly an adolescent. He
needed a father as well as a mother.

She was suddenly overwhelmed by an almost unbearable sadness and regret. Should she have stayed with Geoff for the sake of their son?

For several seconds she let the past spool back in her mind. Then she took a deep breath and went to change into her walking boots. There was no use in trying to alter the past. She had to just learn from it and try harder with the future; that was the only way forward.

★ ★ ★

Saturday was quiet and companionable. Tim was his old sunny self and helped Julie clean and cook for the coming week which he would spend mainly with his father, with her popping in and out when she could take a few hours off from work. Tim fretted because there was no word from his father but Julie assured him he wouldn't let them down.

'Has he ever?' she asked as they sat on the terrace overlooking the village late Sunday morning.

'Apart from not living with us, no, he hasn't.'

'To be accurate and truthful, Tim, *we* left him.'

Tim shrugged. 'Whatever.' He was scanning the sky for birds through binoculars. 'Hey, Mum, I think that's a kestrel. See, up there to the right.' He handed her the glasses.

'You're right. It's beautiful.' The kestrel swooped and Julie followed its flight path towards the track leading to the village, where a straggly party of walkers was coming towards the cottage. She counted ten figures in all, most of them wearing hiking boots, backpacks and sticks.

'There's something familiar about those guys down there. And it looks as though they're coming here.'

'But there's no walking trail to the moors behind us,' Tim said. 'It's the other side of the village. They must be lost.' He tried again to take the glasses from her but Julie fended him off.

'Wait a sec . . . I know them! They're from St Clements! There's Dan at the front and . . . Robert Kendall, your rescuer, and — heavens above . . . Polly Fellowes!'

There were one or two she didn't recognise but it was certainly a group from the hospital and they were heading her way. Dan waved and Tim dashed down to meet them. Julie waved back, unsure of her reaction to the invasion. She had always considered Moorland View her own peaceful sanctuary.

Tim, flanked by Rob and Dan, was chattering excitedly as they neared the cottage: 'It's half-term and my dad's coming from the States any minute now . . . '

'We won't stay long then. Hi, Julie!' Dan went to hug her. 'I hope we're not intruding on your Sunday peace but your cottage was only a short detour on our hike so we thought we'd come and say hello.'

'What a lovely surprise,' she replied.

'I'll put the coffee on. Tim, could you show Dan where the garden chairs are? We can sit outside.'

The rest of the group was gathered on the terrace, shrugging off packs, greeting Julie, explaining and apologising.

'No need, it's good to see you,' she assured them politely. 'I'm glad you caught us in — Tim's father's due any time.'

Like a flock of starlings, the hikers found perches on the low stone walls surrounding the garden. Dan and Tim brought chairs, and Julie carried out a tray with mugs of coffee and biscuits.

'This is such a surprise,' she repeated as she served coffee.

'Blame Rob here,' Dan said. 'He's a great walker apparently, and he's started a sort of St Clements rambling club. This is our first outing and I suppose I have to take the blame for the invasion. You remember last autumn, Julie, you and I, and Tim, went for a walk round Wellsdale and we came back here for supper?'

'It was fun,' Tim said. 'I'll take Dad on that walk. I can remember it.'

'We have all the ordnance survey maps in any case,' Julie said. 'I never took you for a walker, Polly.'

'Well, I do have a life outside St Clements,' Polly protested. 'It was my friend Gary here who persuaded me to come, though.'

Gary, bearded and taciturn, inclined his head slightly.

'Do you work at St Clements?' Julie asked, thinking what an unlikely combination Gary and Polly made.

Gary shook his head briefly and turned away to stare at the view.

'This is a lovely spot.' Rob came to sit next to Julie. 'This invasion is my fault — I told Dan we should have phoned.'

'No, really, it's fine. It's good to have company.'

Rob, casual in shorts, boots and T-shirt, looked entirely different from the busy senior consultant she'd met previously. Relaxed, he stretched out tanned, muscular legs to the sun. 'I wish I could find somewhere like this.' He smiled at Julie. 'You're not thinking of selling up, I suppose?'

'Certainly not. Never, I hope.'

'OK, I wasn't serious.' He put on dark glasses. 'The sun's strong here.'

In truth, Rob was simply using the sunglasses as Julie had the other day — they allowed him to look at her more closely, unobserved. Wearing jeans and T-shirt and with her hair tumbling round her shoulders, she looked a different person from the power-dressed career woman in the Feathers. He was seeking some trace of the young schoolgirl he must have encountered some time at Fletcher Comprehensive. He searched his memory but met a blank. It was her older sister, Olivia, he remembered, though he could see in Julie a family resemblance — the expressive eyes were beautiful.

She was aware of his scrutiny and

turned to talk to Dan.

'We must go bowling again soon,' she said. 'Tim enjoyed it. But another time we'll stick together.'

'Sure. I'll check my schedule,' Dan replied, shading his eyes against the sun. 'There's a car heading this way, just turning into your track.'

Tim leapt to his feet, his face alight with excitement. 'It's Dad. Dad!'

The group on the terrace watched as the car stopped by one of the sheds below the house. A tall, bronzed man wearing jeans, short-sleeved shirt and dark glasses jumped out and opened his arms to Tim who jumped right into them. Boy and man clung together.

Robert watched as Julie moved towards them, smiling broadly.

'Hi,' she called, 'it's good to see you,' and she was enveloped in the family hug.

'It's time we went,' Dan murmured to Robert.

'Sure.' Rob still had his eyes on the group. 'Husband's return? Lucky guy.'

'Eh? No, Geoff's Julie's ex. They're divorced.'

'Really? I didn't know that. Looks like a happy family to me.'

'Oh, they're both potty about Tim.'

'Just about Tim?' queried Rob with a final glance at the good-looking tall blond man and dark-haired Julie, laughing, arm-in-arm, the man's hand on the boy's shoulder.

★　★　★

'They seem a nice bunch of guys,' Geoff remarked as he helped Julie clear the coffee cups.

'They are. I hope you didn't mind them being here, it was totally unexpected.'

'Not at all, it was good to meet them.'

'How long are you staying?' Tim asked eagerly.

'Only a few days.'

The boy's face dropped. 'Aw, you promised longer — a week at least.'

'I know, but I've got great news,' said Geoff. 'I've been moved to San Diego to run the company's west coast operation. It's a big step up and it means I have to go back Thursday *but* the deal is I can be freed up for a couple of extra weeks later in the summer. How's that?'

'We-ell.' Tim considered. 'Not bad I suppose.'

'And you've never visited me in the States, so if your mum agrees, I'd like you to come to California for a visit in late summer. How's that?'

'Wow! California? Can we surf? Go game fishing?'

'I don't see why not. I'm already negotiating half-ownership of a boat, a luxury yacht, which I'll be able to take anywhere in the world.'

Tim's eyes widened further. 'Can I go? Please, Mum?'

'Sounds like an offer you can't refuse.'

'You don't mind, do you, Julie?' Geoff looked anxious. 'You could come along too. You'd be very welcome.'

'I don't think so, not at present. I've too much work on here right now.'

'At the new job? What's it like?'

'I'll tell you later. Right now, Tim's got a full day's programme planned for you.'

'OK, I'm game. Just let me get my bags out of the car.' He put his hands on her shoulders. 'You look great, by the way — you get younger and more beautiful with each visit.'

'You look pretty good yourself.'

'America suits me, and I'm going to love California. The company's booming and I can afford a terrific house, huge pool, a great car.'

Tim helped his father unload the boot.

'Here — take these. Presents.' Geoff gave Tim an armful and handed Julie a couple of gift-wrapped items.

'Thanks, Dad. I'll look at them later. Can we get down to some fishing now? I've got a new rod I want to try.'

Julie was frowning. 'Geoff, you didn't

have to buy me anything.'

'I know I didn't, but I wanted to.' Briefly he touched her arm. 'It's the least I can do.'

'What do you mean?' She was puzzled. Geoff had never brought her presents before. Relations between them had improved a good deal over the years since the divorce and they'd both made great efforts for Tim's sake. When they were all together as a family, an outsider would never have suspected they were divorced.

'I'll just take my bag in then we'll be off.' Geoff ignored Julie's question and followed Tim into the cottage.

★ ★ ★

It was a good day out. They hiked up to a stream Geoff and Tim had discovered on a previous visit. It was Tim who caught most of the fish for supper and Tim who, under supervision, barbecued them for a sunset supper back on the terrace at Moorland View. Later, a sleepy Tim went up to his room to try out the new computer game his dad had brought him while Geoff and Julie sat on over coffee, enjoying the night air.

'Brandy?' Geoff produced his duty-free bottle.

She shook her head. 'I'm driving, but you go ahead.'

'Driving? Where to?'

'Home, of course. I'm working tomorrow.'

'But surely you could go early in the morning. It's not far.'

'I'd rather get back tonight. I'm starting a new project, clinical trials of a new drug. I need to be at work early tomorrow. Besides, the whole idea was for you and Tim to be together. Boys' stuff. Tim's got plans.'

'That's fine, but I thought you'd be around too.'

'I shall — probably Friday. We can have a day all together.'

'I have to fly back on Friday, the new job starts on Monday.'

'I'll take Thursday off then. Tim'll be disappointed you're going so soon.'

'I'll be back in the summer holidays and take him back with me if you agree. Or better still, you could fly out with him and stay a day or two.'

'No I shan't do that.'

Geoff poured himself a brandy and there was silence for a while.

'Er . . . how's Lyndy?' she asked at last.

'Lyndy? She's out of the picture.'

'What? But I — I thought she was the love of your life.'

'That's what I thought at the time but it just didn't work out.'

'Did she . . . has she left you?'

He nodded. 'We're in the process of a divorce right now.'

'Oh, Geoff, I'm sorry.

'Me too. All that hoo-ha between you and me — it's such a pity.'

Julie was silent. Geoff's affair with Lyndy had been the last straw that had finally propelled her back across the Atlantic.

Geoff was looking at her. 'We messed up, Julie, didn't we?'

She could just about see his profile in the gathering darkness and could see well enough what had made her fall in love with him ten years earlier. He was very attractive, the dusk erasing his few faint age lines.

'We were both to blame,' she said briskly, picking up the tray of cups. 'That's all past anyway. Let's go and see what Tim's up to, then I must be making a move.'

He got to his feet. 'Sure you won't stay over? I've a bottle of wine in the car — log fire in the sitting-room . . . '

'Thanks, you make it sound tempting but Monday morning looms.'

'Maybe another time?'

Julie chose to pretend she hadn't heard that question.

A Surprise From Sandra

Julie had to put both Tim and Geoff out of her mind for the next few days. She was sure they would enjoy their rural idyll without her and she felt free to concentrate on work.

Several hospitals in the area suddenly began to show interest in the drug trials. She suspected Eric Lancaster's touch behind the scenes. Maldon's managing director was a local man with many contacts in the area. Before long, Julie had sorted out eight hospitals suitable for running the trials, including top-of-the-list St Clements.

There was a lot of paper shuffling first though, and the trials' start could yet be weeks away.

Much as she loved him, she was glad Tim was at Moorland View. It meant she was able to work through the evenings.

The evening before she was to return to Moorland View, she was finishing off some paperwork. Her fingers flew over the keyboard, facts and figures aligning themselves in her head. She was about to wrap it up when Sandra knocked on her door.

'Hi, Mum, come in. I've just a little bit more to do, then . . .'

Her mother backed away. 'Tomorrow will do. I don't want to disturb you. Have you eaten?'

'Not yet.' Julie looked at her watch. 'Goodness! It's nearly ten. I'll put the kettle on.' She stretched and yawned. 'I'll have an early night, I think. I'm off to Moorland View to collect Tim tomorrow.'

'I saw your light was on very late last night. I couldn't sleep myself so I was up.'

'I was working. Much as I miss Tim, he has so much homework now that it's been good to have a free stretch of time to work on my project.'

'You're still enjoying it?'

'Yes,' Julie agreed, saving her work and shutting down the laptop. 'It's great to have total responsibility for a big project though I suspect Eric is keeping a watchful eye from the sidelines. It's all coming together very well. Mum, is something the matter? You seem a bit . . . edgy.'

'No, not really but . . . um . . . '

'Do you have a migraine coming on?'

'No, no, it's nothing like that. I miss Tim . . . and Sam and Eddie.' Julie's brothers were away on a last bachelor holiday together. 'Maybe you . . . one day . . . '

Julie was bewildered. 'Where would I go?'

'Well, new job, new people — and you're such an attractive woman . . . '

Julie groaned. 'Please, not that again. For the last time, I'm happy, busy, content. Please, stop worrying about me.'

'I'm not worrying about you, dear. Me — not you. It's me. I'm worried *about me.*'

'You? Why are you worried? You're not ill, are you?'

'No. I told you, I'm fine. But I've been thinking about the future — *my* future, here in Hemsdale. Remember last Sunday? It was a lovely day — Sam's engagement, Ed and his new girl. Your plans to take Tim to Italy, visit your father . . . '

'You said you didn't mind.'

'I don't mind. Truly. You should see your father. I've been selfish. It was wrong . . . '

'So you'll come to Sam's wedding?'

'I didn't say that. I just said I've been thinking a lot about my future. Oh, I'm busy enough, meals on wheels, the charity shop, helping out with family, you and Tim, but you've got your own lives. I've always known that, but on Sunday it suddenly hit me; this can't last for ever, things change and one has to be prepared to welcome change.

'Jane's from the West Country and Sam loves going there — he helps out with Jane's parents' garden centre. They may settle there, it's a beautiful part of the country.

'And look at Eddie. He's restless, I can tell; he flits from girl to girl, doesn't like his job, talks about New Zealand, and he's hardly ever here. You and Tim, too; Tim will grow up fast and once he's at Fletcher . . .'

'We'll both still need you.'

'And I'll always be here for you, wherever I'm living.'

'Wherever? You're thinking of moving?'

'No, not for a while, but this house is far too big even with you and Tim in the flat upstairs.'

'But it's our family home.'

'I know, and I'm not about to sell up next week, but I must have a serious think about the future. I need a change, new avenues to explore . . .'

'Oh, Mum.' Julie gave Sandra a hug. 'I didn't realise. I'm — we're all selfish pigs.'

'No, you're not, you're young people with your own lives to live. I've leaned on you all far too long.'

'No, you've supported us wonderfully, especially me and Tim. We've all just taken you for granted. What can we do for you now?'

'Nothing. It's time I did something for myself. I've already made a tentative move. I hope you'll approve.' She opened her bag and pulled out some brochures and leaflets. 'See what you think.'

Julie skimmed through them: 'Gosh, 'life enhancing', 'life changing', 'adventure learning', 'pathway to a new life: computing, cookery, painting'. You don't need cookery and you're OK with computers. Tim thinks you're a whizz.'

'Tim thinks anybody over fifty who can switch on a computer is a bit rare, bless him. And it's not cookery, it's catering management.'

'Catering?' Julie turned the pages of a glossy publication. 'What a beautiful spot, near Perigord, Southern France . . .'

'Part holiday,' Sandra cut in quickly, 'part a dip into learning. You know I never finished college. I did one year and then I met Carlo. I'd done part of my language course: six months in Italy. Ironic really. Once I met your father, all desire for study vanished..

'I've always wanted to run a small business,' Sandra went on, a new brisk sort of Sandra. 'Even a bed and breakfast would be fun and we're ideally placed here, with loads of tourists in the summer. Barbara's game to come with me. She needs a change too, now her children have gone.'

'Auntie Bee!' Julie was amazed. Barbara Sanders, her mother's friend from primary school days, had six children and had been completely dominated by her old-fashioned husband, Bernard. While he went on business trips all over the world, her horizon had barely extended beyond holidays in Devon with the children.

'Now Bernard's dead she's free to do as she likes. He left her plenty of money, so she's well off and free. She can spread her wings now.'

Julie was reeling. 'We must call a family council.'

'Not necessary, dear. I need to make my own plans, though I'd welcome your approval. Bee found some more information on the internet — she really *is* a whizz at that. We've booked a month in September. Here — ' she passed a brochure to Julie ' — Chateau du Foret, somewhere south of the Dordogne; magnificent grounds, lake, spa, learning or leisure, food and wine, computer, pottery . . .'

'You've booked it?'

'Yes. Bee was so excited, I couldn't stop her, and I suddenly thought, well, why not? To be honest I have been a bit of a stick-in-the-mud — all that terrible depression when Carlo left, and Olivia's miscarriage too.'

'Oh, Mum.' Tears sprang to Julie's eyes. 'Of course you haven't been a stick-in-the-mud! Anything but. And Tim and I would have been lost without you.' She hugged her mother tightly. 'I'm glad for you — it'll be a great adventure.'

'Yes, and the lovely bit is that it will be *my* adventure, my own personal odyssey. Is that selfish?'

'Not a bit, but anyway, it's time you were selfish. I'll get the wine and we'll drink a toast to Sandra Balboni's own odyssey.'

'Thanks. I'll quickly phone Bee. She'll be so excited — she was scared you would disapprove.'

Her mother left the room, leaving a rather chastened Julie wondering what sort of picture Auntie Bee had formed of Sandra's family. Selfish lot of pigs probably, she thought, and it was a salutary lesson.

A slight shiver went through her as she thought of her own future in, say, twenty years, with Tim grown up and away with his own family. Olivia would, she hoped, have more children and Julie herself would be the maiden aunt! The optimist in her pushed the thought away. There were lots of challenges ahead, plenty of time, anything could happen. Still, her mother's news had been a bit of a shock.

*   *   *

Tim's time at Moorland View had been a great success; he'd enjoyed having his father's undivided attention and had looked woebegone when they'd seen Geoff off at the airport.

In the airport lounge Geoff had hugged them both.

'I'll be back soon,' he'd promised Tim, and then he'd turned to Julie. 'Think about a trip to California,' he'd said softly. 'Give it a chance.'

Ignoring his invitation, she had said, 'Tim will love it. It'll be a fabulous adventure for him.' She'd turned her cheek for his goodbye kiss. 'Take care, Geoff. Come on, Tim, time to go.'

Despite his disappointment over his father's early departure, Tim appeared to settle down. He was looking forward to secondary school in September. His class had visited the school and he'd been intrigued to see Julie Balboni's name on a board as a senior prefect of her year.

'I liked Fletcher,' he told her after his day at the school, 'but I could go to school in California. Dad says I could take up surfing as a sports subject.'

'Did he indeed? That's a bit difficult in Hemsdale. Fletcher has a good sports range; lots of adventure camping in the Dales.'

'Uh huh,' Tim was immersed in his computer and refused to look at her.

She began to realise she may have the beginnings of a problem with him. Visions of a glamorous Californian lifestyle could well present difficulties. Maybe it wasn't such a good idea for him to visit America. But then, Geoff was his father and the one thing they'd both agreed on was that the most important person in the triangle was Tim, and both parents were to have an equal say in his future.

Fortunately Julie was absorbed by work, and an invitation to supper at

Professor Rutherford's house made a welcome social break.

'It'll do you good,' Sandra said, delighted to keep an eye on Tim. 'You don't get out enough.'

She nodded approvingly as Julie came downstairs dressed to go out.

'You look lovely. I do like your hair loose instead of scraped back. Have a good time. Dan's driving you, isn't he?'

'Mmm, it's his turn, and he wants to show off his new car.'

'He's a nice man. You're . . . um . . . good friends?'

'Yes — and that's all, so you can put that idea out of your head.'

'What idea, dear?' Sandra looked innocent as a car's horn tooted outside.

* * *

In retirement Will and Kathy Rutherford were enjoying inviting friends and former colleagues to informal suppers at their large family house on the outskirts of Hemsdale.

'Julie,' Kathy Rutherford greeted her in the hall, 'you look stunning. The new job evidently agrees with you.'

'And retirement suits you.' The two women hugged as the professor came to join them.

'Welcome, my dear — and you too, Dan. Come on in, I think everyone's here now.'

He led them through to a drawing-room where Julie was surprised to see both Rob Kendall and Polly Fellowes standing by the fireplace, drinks in hand, Polly looking rather flushed. Julie recognised a couple of St Clements' people, but most of the others she didn't know.

'Champagne, Julie?' Kathy handed her a glass.

'Goodness. Is it a birthday?'

'No, but it's a sort of 'farewell-for-a-bit party'. Will and I have finally booked our retirement round-the-world trip. Now, I think you know a lot of people here but Paul Coogan's over there — I believe he's taking part in

113

your trials. Have you met?'

'No, we've only spoken on the phone. I'd like to meet him.'

'No shop, mind. Paul's a great fell walker, knows the area round your cottage very well.'

Paul Coogan was a consultant at Julie's most distant trials hospital and she was delighted to meet him and his wife. They were seated together at the supper table and in spite of Kathy Rutherford's injunction, they were able to talk shop and clarify one or two points.

The evening flew by. After supper, coffee was served in the living-room. Once or twice, Julie saw Rob move towards her but each time he was waylaid by someone wanting to talk to him. She noticed Polly Fellowes arguing with a couple of people. She seemed to be drinking more than usual. Finally one or two guests began to leave and Julie looked at her watch in surprise — she hadn't realised the time.

'You're not leaving, I hope.' Rob appeared at her side. 'I've been trying to talk to you all evening.' He looked relaxed and handsome in open-necked shirt and casual trousers. 'It's good to be out of the hospital. Can I get you some wine?'

'No, thanks. I ought to be going, I've left Tim with my mother.'

'How is Tim? Did he have a good week with his dad?'

'Oh, yes, they . . .'

An anxious-looking Dan interrupted. 'Julie, I'm worried about Polly. She shouldn't drive. Her home's on my route back and I could take her, but it's a bit out of our way for you.'

'No problem,' Rob said swiftly, 'I'd be happy to take Julie. Is that OK by you, Julie? I live not far from you. In fact, I met your mother the other day in the supermarket. I remembered her from schooldays. She was on the P.T.A. I was the student representative at some of their meetings. I think I only volunteered hoping for access to your sister through your mum. Fat chance of that!'

'What's going on?' Polly joined them, glass in hand. 'And who's taking me home? The professor says it's best to leave my car here. I disagree but it's been a great party. Rob, is it OK for Dan to take me home?'

'Of course; he's already offered and you're on his way. It'll be more convenient if I take Julie.'

'Whatever.' Polly yawned and linked arms with Dan. 'Lead on, Prince Charming. I shall probably sleep all the way home.'

'See you, Julie, Rob.' Dan steered Polly away.

'Ready?' Rob asked.

Julie nodded. 'That's really not like Polly. I thought she was practically teetotal,' she commented.

'I don't know her very well but there are hospital rumours of a difficult boyfriend.'

'She was divorced a few years back and suffered depression for a while afterwards. But she bounced back and threw herself into her work. She wanted your job, I expect you know that.'

They went to say their goodbyes to their hosts, and Julie bid them a fond farewell.

'Come and see us with travellers' tales when you get back.' She kissed them both. 'I'll miss you.'

Will put his arm round his wife's shoulders. 'We're going to have a wonderful time.'

As they drove away Julie said, 'If anyone deserves a good retirement they do. They've just had their golden wedding. Fifty years — imagine.'

'That's quite an achievement.'

They drove in silence for a while. She felt sleep creeping over her and was stifling a yawn when Rob stopped the car.

'This is where I live. Not far from you. Can I . . . would you like a quick coffee, or is it too late? There are a couple of things I'd like to clear up on the trials. I know now's not the time, but I'm usually snowed under at the hospital.'

'Sure. It's not all that late — we did have an early start to the evening.'

He'd pulled up at an imposing three-storey Victorian terrace house. Julie was curious to see where Rob lived. Would there be a watchful wife peering through the window? Somehow it didn't seem likely.

'Ground-floor flat.' He inserted his key in the door. 'Temporary rented accommodation.'

There was no anxious wife and the spacious flat had an impersonal bach-elor feel about it.

'Make yourself comfortable, I'll put the kettle on.'

There was a big sofa, two deep armchairs, a low table covered in books and papers, and a corner desk housing a computer. He went to the desk and handed her a sheet of paper.

'This is Polly's proposed letter telling pregnant women about the trials and inviting them to take part. I'd be grateful if you'd cast your eye over it. It seems a bit . . . clinical to me.'

She skimmed through the letter and realised that Rob was right: it was brusque and the tone was much too clinical. She picked up a pen and circled a couple of phrases, and pencilled in a couple of sentences that would help patients' understanding of the trials.

Rob was still in the kitchen. She looked around the room, bare of ornaments, a couple of framed photographs on the mantelpiece. She went to examine them; one was of a large group with Rob near the centre. It was a fairly recent picture of him, taken in summer. His arms were linked with an elderly white-haired couple. Everyone was smiling, and there was a large white marquee in the background. Obviously a happy day!

'That's my parents' golden wedding last summer — the Rutherfords aren't the only ones to make it.' Rob pushed aside papers and magazines to put a coffee tray on the low table. 'I came back from Ghana for the party. It was a great weekend; we hadn't had a family get-together for ages.'

'Do you have a large family?'

'One brother, two sisters, all younger than me and scattered around England, one in the States. How about you? I know about your sister, Olivia, of course.'

'We have twin brothers, Sam and Eddie, who are younger than me. Our parents divorced ten years ago. Dad remarried in Italy and has two young children. My family all live locally. Mum took the divorce hard but I think she's about to start a new life: she's off to France in September on a new learning curve.'

'Good for her. And you? Tim's dad was at your cottage the other Sunday.'

'We divorced six years ago.'

'He seemed a nice guy,' Rob remarked as he poured coffee into mugs.

'Yes.'

'I'm sorry — about the divorce, I mean. You seemed like a good family.'

'Well, appearances can be deceptive, can't they?' She put her cup down, suddenly angry with herself for coming here. There had been no need, he could just as easily have e-mailed Polly's letter.

'I have to go, it's late. I've made a couple of amendments to Polly's letter, just a few suggestions. Feel free to ignore them.'

'You haven't drunk your coffee.'

'No. I don't think I want it after all.'

He looked puzzled; her sudden hostility was palpable. 'I hope I haven't upset you. I didn't mean to pry into your divorce. I'm sorry.'

'It's all right,' she said brusquely, 'but if you'd take me home now, or I can phone for a taxi . . .'

'I'll take you, of course.' He was angry, too, now, unable to understand her changed mood. The air between them sparked.

She shrugged on her jacket. The

evening had been so pleasant, she'd actually forgotten the hurtful words he'd uttered those many years ago. Now they came flooding back; could she ever forget them?

As for her divorce, she would probably never have married Geoff at the ridiculously early age of seventeen had it not been for Robert Kendall, head boy at Fletcher Comprehensive.

Family Plans

'These trials are going too well,' Julie confided to her secretary, Lucy, one sunny summer morning a few weeks later.

'Don't speak too soon. Mr Courtney at Oxdales wants to talk to you.'

'He might spell trouble but I think he's a good guy at heart. Apparently his sister lost a baby in premature labour years ago so he has a personal interest, which is good. I'll call him right away.'

'And your sister phoned. Can you call her back?'

'I'll talk to Mr Courtney first.'

Mr Courtney turned out to be as sweet as pie. He was an old-fashioned consultant who insisted on calling his patients by their full names and that courtesy extended to Julie.

'Mrs Haywood,' he boomed down the phone. 'Thanks for calling back so promptly. I've a slight worry about one of my patients who wants to volunteer for the trial . . . '

He outlined his concerns, and asked if Julie could offer any ideas.

When she had presented a considered view, he sounded approving.

'Excellent. Thank you. Oh, and I've looked at your adjustments to my management strategy and I agree with all your suggestions. Eric Lancaster tells me it's your first major project? Well done so far.'

'Thank you, Mr Courtney, I appreciate your saying that.'

She felt a glow of satisfaction as she hung up.

Eric Lancaster came into her office ten minutes later.

'I hear you've got Fred Courtney eating out of your hand. I met him at the golf club yesterday and he was singing your praises.' He perched on the edge of her desk. 'You seem to have this project well under control though it's early stages yet, but if you want to take in another area there's a possible link-up with your S.A.D. work. Some guy in America has written a paper on it.'

'Interesting, but I'd like to see this one through a bit farther if that's OK.'

'Fine. How's it going at St Clements?'

Julie flushed. She hadn't seen Robert Kendall since that night she'd been to his flat. In retrospect, she was ashamed of her surge of anger. It was stupid to harbour any feeling of resentment over such a small, longpast incident. The problem was, it hadn't been a small matter to her at the time. Maybe she could confront him with it and clear the air . . .

Eric was speaking, looking at her desk calendar.

'So it may be at the end of September, maybe later, but staff will be notified well in advance,' he was saying.

'What? Sorry, Eric, what were you saying?'

'Maldon's — established twenty-five years ago this year. The board thinks a celebration is in order, especially since some of us, myself included, have been with the firm since it started.'

'Really? Twenty-five years? You can't be that old surely?'

He laughed. 'Flattery will get you everywhere, Julie. Perhaps you could contribute a few ideas as to the nature of the occasion?'

'I'll give it some thought, though with Sam and Jane's wedding coming up, my brain will be going into overload with party plans.'

'How is the family? Tim's about to start secondary school, isn't he? That'll be a big change.'

'Yes, he's growing up fast. He's going to spend time in California with his father in the summer. It'll be good for him to experience life outside Hemsdale. He barely remembers his early years in the States.'

'I'm sure he'll have a great time.' Eric patted her shoulder. 'Keep up the good work, but don't drive yourself too hard.'

He hovered in the doorway as though he wanted to say more, thought better of it and walked away.

Eric Lancaster was a managing director who took a personal interest in his staff. He'd known Julie long enough and well enough to notice signs of strain. His own daughter was a single parent and he knew it wasn't easy. He resolved to make the Maldon's anniversary party an event to remember.

★ ★ ★

Towards the end of the day, Julie phoned Olivia. 'How are things? I got your message, but I'll phone from home this evening for a longer chat. I'm a bit pushed right now, I've got to meet Tim and . . . '

'You're always too busy to talk to me. Surely you're interested in your niece or nephew?' There was a note of petulance in Olivia's voice.

'Of course I am. Is there anything wrong?'

'No, but Michael's away for a couple of nights. I wondered if you could come over tonight or tomorrow.'

'I can't really. Tim's got a friend coming for a sleepover and I'm meeting Sam and Jane for a pub supper on Sunday to discuss wedding plans. Why don't you join us? Come and stay with me while Michael's away.'

'I can't leave the dogs, and I don't feel up to that much company.'

'You're all right though?' Julie asked anxiously. 'Anyway, it's family — hardly company. Nothing wrong medically?'

'No. I'm just a bit . . . oh, never mind, if you're busy, you're busy.'

'Ellena's there?'

'I suppose so, though she's hardly company.'

'I'll come over on Saturday. Perhaps we can walk the dogs and have lunch.'

'Can't Mum keep an eye on Tim and his sleepover mate?'

'Mum's away for the weekend.'

'Away? But she never goes away!'

'Well, she's about to start. She and Auntie Bee are going on a bridge weekend.'

'Bridge? She's never played bridge.'

'It's a beginners' weekend. In York.'

There was a long pause, during which Lucy came in with a pile of letters. Julie gestured for her to leave them on the desk.

'Anyway, you will come to our Midsummer Eve party, won't you?' Olivia persisted. 'You won't be too busy for that?'

'Of course not, have I ever missed it? And, Olivia, if you don't feel well — you know, before Saturday — I'll come straight over.'

'All right. See you,' and Olivia put the phone down, her tone implying that, no, it certainly was not all right, and Julie sighed. She knew she would have to call in on her sister before she went home that evening.

As it happened, when she did call in at Pendale Court, two of Olivia's girlfriends were there, one cooking supper, the other staying the night to keep Olivia company.

Julie had coffee with them then left for home with a clear conscience.

Olivia looked blooming as she hugged her goodbye.

'I'm glad you came. Sorry I was a bit of a wimp earlier but I do get anxious when I'm on my own. Mike's arranging to be here as much as he cam, bless him, so I'll be OK.'

'Are the hospital appointments going well?'

'Marvellous.' Her eyes lit up. 'Rob Kendall is so good, so reassuring. I've begged him to be around for the delivery.'

'Olivia, you can't do that.'

'Can't I?' Olivia grinned mischievously. 'Just watch me. He's coming to our midsummer party. He told me he had a crush on me at Fletcher, can you believe that? I hardly remember him.' She kissed Julie's cheek briefly. 'Take care. Keep me up to date with the wedding plans — and you must tell me what Mum's up to.'

'I will. It's good. I'll ring you over the weekend.'

★ ★ ★

Sam Balboni raised his tanned face to the sun, took a gulp of his pint and exhaled slowly.

'It seems odd not to be at Mum's for Sunday lunch. Have you heard from her, Ju?'

'She phoned last night, having a wonderful time apparently — lovely hotel, interesting people. She's booked in again in three weeks' time.'

'Good for her,' Jane said. 'It's good that she's having a break.'

'Change of life more like.' Eddie lazily flicked stones into the river. They'd driven out to a favourite country pub by a river, the excuse for the outing to discuss plans for Sam and Jane's wedding. Jane was going back home the following weekend to talk to her parents about their plans.

'We need a firm date first.' She had a checklist in front of her.

'That's up to you.' Sam leaned over to kiss her. 'I'm happy with whatever you decide. Is late August too soon? It's only going to be family and few friends.'

'That's what you think,' Eddie teased.

'Tim's in America in August,' Julie said.

'I don't mind, honest.' Tim was sprawled on the grass playing with Eddie's much-spoilt bearded collie.

'But we want you to dress up as a page-boy: satin suit, bow tie, frilly shirt.' Eddie was in a teasing mood.

Tim glared at his uncle. 'Then I'm definitely not coming.'

'You know he's only kidding,' Jane soothed.

Sandwiches and wine arrived at their table and talk drifted off the wedding and on to other topics. The main discussion was Sandra Balboni's sudden bid for independence. They all agreed it was a good thing and not before time but they were all aware of just a hint of dismay that the mother hen was leaving the coop before her chicks were quite ready to let her go — despite the fact that all of the Balboni 'children' were fully-fledged adults with lives of their own.

Sam was the first to articulate the feeling. 'I suppose it's because Mum's always been there.'

'But actually, as far as I remember, when Dad left, it was Julie who kept us all together,' Eddie said. 'Mum collapsed into a depressed heap and Olivia was demented and had a miscarriage.'

'She had a premature baby that died,' Julie corrected.

'Whatever. She wasn't a lot of use, was she?'

'Why *did* Dad leave Mum?' Eddie asked. 'I can't remember much. Sam and I were only ten and nobody would talk about it. Dad was just the bad guy who'd left us all for a younger, more glamorous woman.'

'Younger, yes; we don't know about the glamorous.'

'She's . . . Isabella . . . is very pretty,' Julie said.

Sam frowned. 'How do you know?'

'I've been in touch. He sent photographs. He's desperate to see us all.'

'No way.' Sam was adamant.

Eddie backed him up. 'How could you, Ju? Have you told Mum, or Olivia? She hates him.'

'She doesn't *know* him. None of you do.'

The argument raged and only Jane was quiet — and Tim, carefully pretending to be occupied with the dog whilst following every word.

'I think you should ask him to our wedding,' Jane put in.

'Mum wouldn't like . . . ' said Sam.

'Mum would hate it,' said Eddie.

'I'm not so sure,' Julie said slowly. 'She's changing, getting a life. She doesn't mind if I go visit him in Italy with Tim.'

There was a startled silence, then Jane spoke quickly. 'I'll be Jane Balboni soon and I think I'd like to meet my father-in-law to be.'

'And he's my grandad,' Tim announced as he stood up, 'so if Mum'll take me, I'd like to go to Rome.'

Julie smiled at Tim, grateful for his support. 'He's opened another restaurant in Florence.'

'I've always wanted to go to Florence,' Jane said, taking Sam's hand.

'Coffee all round?' asked Julie.

Eddie was confused. 'Seems like a betrayal to me.'

'What was he like? He was away a lot before he finally left us. I never really knew him.' Sam was interested in spite of himself.

'He was fun,' Julie told him. 'A big, laughing dark-haired guy when I was small — then a sort of sadness flushed out the laughter and he and Mum were always rowing. He wanted her and us to go to Italy with him.'

'Did he?' Eddie looked surprised. 'I thought he just met this younger girl and shoved off, leaving us to sink or swim.'

'That's because we didn't dare mention him. Mum would just cry and cry — so we all wiped him out of our lives.'

'Until now?' Jane put her arm round Sam and touched Eddie's hand. 'Maybe . . . at least you should hear his side of the story.'

Coffee arrived, harmony followed, and it was eventually decided that Sam, Jane, Julie and Tim should all go to Italy. Sam would book a weekend package break to Florence if Julie would check that was where he was living at the moment, and they would visit Carlo Balboni and his family during the break. As Jane pointed out, that way, if it all fell to pieces, at least they would have the hotel to return to.

Julie's spirits lifted and she felt excited at the prospect of seeing her father. Sam caught the atmosphere and promised to make the booking after checking his diary dates. Only Eddie looked doubtful. 'I think you'd better check with Olivia — she'll have something to say.'

'She should have come today then. You did invite her, Julie?'

'Of course I did, but then, I didn't know a visit to Dad was on the agenda.'

'I think you did. You were always the sly one . . . '

The Balbonis bickered amicably for another hour or so until they all parted with hugs and kisses and promises to be in touch again soon.

'And of course, there's still Olivia's midsummer party to come,' Eddie said. 'That's always fun.'

'No Vanda today?' Julie commented to Sam as they watched Eddie roar out of the car park in his latest sports car.

'She's working, and anyway, she's not exactly part of the family — yet,' said Sam, 'though I do think he's pretty smitten this time.'

Traditionally Olivia's and Michael's midsummer party was held on the nearest Saturday to Midsummer Day itself. This year, on the morning of the party, a torrential thunderstorm threatened to write off the idea of early drinks and nibbles outdoors, but by afternoon the skies were clear and the strong sun dried up the manicured lawns sufficiently to set up tables and chairs around the gardens and flower beds.

By early evening, champagne and savouries were circulating among the many guests. Michael had lots of business associates as well as many friends in the area and nobody wanted to miss the party of the year.

Olivia was in her element, already showing her coming baby and positively glowing with health.

'You look so well.' Julie raised her glass of champagne. 'Here's to infant power. Any names yet?'

'No. I feel that would be tempting

fate,' Olivia commented.

'You'll be fine,' Rob Kendall said, joining the sisters. 'Wonderful garden, Olivia. Do you do it yourself?'

'Heavens, no!. Michael has a troop of gardeners. Can't you tell?' She leaned over and kissed Rob on the cheek. 'Thanks for coming. Julie thought it wasn't a good idea — unprofessional, she said, but you've known Michael for years, haven't you?'

'I knew him in the third form at Fletcher before he and his family moved south. We ran into each other in London some years ago and we've kept in touch.'

'Well, anyway, I'm very happy to see you here. Michael's going to get the barbecue started for the kids and we'll have supper indoors. See you later — I must go and talk to our new neighbours.'

Rob turned to Julie as Olivia left. 'So, you think it's unprofessional to come to a social event where the hostess is a patient?'

She flushed. 'I don't think it's a good thing.'

'I told you, I was madly in love with your sister at school — she was unbelievably glamorous. I remember she played Juliet in the school play and I went to see it every night. She's still a very attractive woman.'

'Mmm. How's the pregnancy going?'

He laughed. 'How very unprofessional, Mrs Haywood! You know I can't discuss a patient's condition with anyone. But she's fine. Can I get you a refill?' he offered.

'Why not? Tim and I are staying overnight tonight, so yes, thank you.'

However, it was some time before Julie got her champagne refill as she was press-ganged into barbecue supervision and every time she had a glimpse of Rob, Olivia was hanging on his every word. Michael was doing much more mixing and socialising with the guests.

The party's official end was marked as usual by a sparkling display of fireworks to celebrate the longest day of the year. After that people began to drift away. Julie was helping Michael clear away the barbecue when Rob finally appeared at her elbow, glass in hand.

'Am I too late with this? I'm so sorry, I was sort of delayed and then Mike and I snatched a minute to talk about finance.'

He held out the glass, smiling, his tanned forearm a striking contrast against his white shirt. Julie was mesmerised. In the half light from the garden lanterns, she saw again that younger Robert Kendall she'd adored with all the agony of its unrequited impossibilities.

She shook her head and waved away the glass Rob was offering. 'No, thanks. I've got to find Tim.' Turning away, she ran towards the house.

'Julie, what's wrong?' she heard Rob call. He started to follow her but she slipped in a side door before he could catch her.

It was the first time in years that Sandra Balboni had missed Olivia's party. She'd been away on a weekend bridge course with her friend, Bee. Julie looked forward to hearing about her weekend, but felt apprehensive about her own news regarding the trip to Italy.

After a lazy and very late brunch on Sunday morning at Pendale Court, she and Tim drove home.

'Gran's home,' said Tim as they turned into the drive. 'I wonder if she's won any cups yet?'

Julie laughed. 'It's a bit early for that. It was a beginners' weekend.'

'That doesn't matter, beginners can win cups for the best beginner.'

'You're quite right,' she agreed. 'Tim, don't tell Granny about Italy straight away. Let's hear about her weekend first.'

'Quite right,' Tim echoed with a cheeky smile, and Julie felt a wave of love for her bright son. She would miss him terribly when he went to stay with Geoff.

Sandra met them at the door, smiling broadly.

'Mum! Did you have a good time?'

'I did, it was lovely. And guess what . . .'

Tim smirked. 'You won the best beginner's cup.'

'Yes, I did! How on earth ..?'

Tim tapped the side of his head. 'Brains,' he chortled, 'on my granny's side — inherited genius.'

Sandra laughed as she hugged him.

'Come on in, I've made us some tea. Tell me how the party went. I was sorry to miss it but I've been to lots before and it was a nice change for Bee, too. Durham's a lovely city. Shall we have tea in the garden? It's far too nice for indoors. You had a good day for the party. How's Olivia?'

Julie followed them indoors, happy for her mother — she hadn't seen her so animated for years.

Over tea and flapjacks (bought in

143

York, not home-made for the first time ever), mother and daughter exchanged their weekend news.

'Olivia is blooming. She was the life and soul on Saturday but a bit tired today. I left her in bed,' Julie confided.

'I'll pop round and see her tomorrow. She's very keen on Rob Kendall as her consultant, isn't she? Mind you, he's a lovely man; I had quite a chat with him the other day in town. Now, he's an attractive man, and I hear he's working with you?'

'Yes, Mum, but I want to talk about Italy.' She spoke very quickly to douse the speculative gleam in Sandra's eyes.

'Yes, dear. Did I tell you Bee and I are thinking of a trip to London next weekend? It's time I went shopping. I felt quite shabby next to Bee this weekend. So I'll be away all weekend, is that OK? You don't want me to look after Tim?'

'No. In fact we'll be away too. You did say it was all right for us to visit Dad?'

'Of course, though I didn't realise it

would be so soon.'

'I didn't either, but Sam got a good deal on the flights. He and Jane are coming too.'

Sandra's surprise was plain. 'Sam's going? To see his father?'

'To be honest I think Jane gave him the push — she's dying to go to Florence and that's where Dad is at the moment. We're on a package — a posh hotel in the centre — so we won't stay long at Dad's.'

'You've no need to worry, Julie, I'm quite happy for you to go, and with Sam and Jane going too, it'll be fun.'

Julie breathed a sigh of relief. Her mother seemed relaxed about it.

'Florence? I thought he lived in Rome?' she asked.

'He's opened a new restaurant in Florence. They've got an apartment nearby. We're just going to . . . er . . . just pop in and see them.'

'I hope you'll do more than that. Be sure to take your camera. I think I'd like to see where he lives now, and maybe a picture of his children. You never know, once Bee and I start our European tour, we might be glad of a recommended restaurant in Florence, so you must go for a meal. Now, I'll just make a quick call to Bee, I think I know where we went wrong during the last hand of bridge we played. But don't go away, I've lots more to tell you.'

A Trip To Italy

'Wow!' Sam Balboni gasped as he took in the spectacular view. The tour bus had parked high above the city to let the tourists take in the whole panorama of Florence straddling the River Arno. Tim chattered with delight as he scanned the scene through Sam's binoculars.

Julie sighed, feeling herself relax. Arriving in the balmy dusk the previous evening, they'd spent a lazy few hours strolling the busy streets, eating pizza or pasta, sipping wine, drinking coffee, watching people saunter by, tourists and Florentines happily mingling in the promenade.

She had called Carlo as soon as they arrived. He had insisted they all come to his restaurant for lunch the next day.

Sam had booked a two-hour morning tour and the panoramic view of the city was their first stop. Feeling the hot sun on her back, a light breeze soothing her shoulders, blue Mediterranean sky above her head, Julie felt happy, relaxed and in holiday mood. She should make the effort to get away more, she decided. She couldn't remember when she'd last had a holiday in the sun.

The tour group moved down to the main square and she enjoyed watching Tim's reactions. He was wide-eyed as he walked the narrow streets with shuttered windows and flower-decked balconies. Here and there they had teasing glimpses of pink and white marble which in the main square turned out to be a huge cathedral with amazing facades and towers.

The square was packed with tourists gazing up at the buildings, photographing the marble statues or just simply staring at the magnificence all around them. Their tour guide led them inside the Duomo and pointed out the tombs of Michael Angelo, Dante, and Galileo. There were so many tour groups it was hard to hear everything their guide was saying.

'I'd love to come back out of season,' Jane whispered. 'It's hard to take it all in.'

Back outside, blinking in the strong sunlight, Sam and Jane lingered on the Ponte Vecchio, the only remaining original bridge over the River Arno. The smart jewellers' shops there drew Sam and Jane like magnets. Their Italian guide told them that originally all the shops had been butchers but 'too smelly', so they had been replaced with jewellers.

Sam put his arms around Jane.

'We haven't chosen an engagement ring yet. Let's see what's on the Ponte Vecchio — it would be a lovely souvenir.'

Jane was starry-eyed. 'Oh, Sam, what a wonderful idea.'

'Maybe we should split up,' Julie suggested. 'The tour's almost finished now. I'll take Tim back to the main square, we'll have a coffee or an ice-cream then meet you outside Dad's restaurant. About twelve-thirty? You've got directions, Sam?'

'Yes. But let's all go into the restaurant together. I'm beginning to feel a bit nervous about seeing him. I probably won't recognise him.'

Julie and Tim continued to wander the streets, concentrating on the quieter back alleys away from the main tourist drag. They went into a small church, sitting for a while in its cool darkness, which was a relief after the hot and crowded main square. Tim was even interested in a small gallery of old paintings.

They bought some postcards and read some potted history notes on the tremendous explosion of talent in Renaissance Italy. Tim pronounced it 'jolly interesting' but he was beginning to feel peckish.

'I think we should go to Grandpa Carlo's now. We've still got to find it. We're not lost, are we?'

'No. Trust me.' Julie studied the

street map her father had faxed. 'Here, see — along this street, through the square and it's ringed in red. We're quite close.' She glanced at her watch. 'It's only just after twelve o'clock. Bags of time.'

'I like it here, it's so different from Hemsdale. I like it being so old. I've seen pictures but actually being here's great. I like the water.'

'You should see Venice then. We could ride a gondola.'

'Can we really come back?'

'I don't see why not, though you've a pretty packed schedule this summer: school adventure camp before you break up, California, then starting your new school.'

Tim smiled and Julie's heart contracted. He was a good-looking boy, well on the way to becoming an attractive young man, and with Geoff's blond good looks combined with his dark Italian eyes he would be a stunner. She put an arm round his shoulders and felt a pang as she realised that she was only two inches taller than him now. Her grip tightened. Once at secondary school he would naturally start growing away from her.

Suddenly she had an irrational longing for another child, a larger family. Childhood disappeared all too quickly.

Tim ducked away from her. 'Come on, let's go. Do you think Grandpa Carlo makes his own pasta? Liam's mum tried it once, but it was a disaster.'

'I'd be surprised if he doesn't.' Julie was studying the map and pointed. 'Through that archway, I think, then we'll soon see the road.'

Sam and Jane were already sitting in the pavement café, heads close together. They both looked up as Julie and Tim came to their table. Jane held out her left hand to display the most beautiful ring, a star sapphire surrounded by tiny diamonds in a thick circle of gold. The setting was old-fashioned, ornate and lovely.

'It's not new but I loved it as soon as

I saw it,' said Jane. 'The jeweller assured me it has a happy past. It had been sold by a wealthy banker's ex-mistress . . . '

Sam hooted. 'If you believe that you'll believe anything! But it will certainly have a happy future.' He kissed her and Tim groaned.

'Aw, come on, Uncle Sam, cut it out! I'm starving and what — '

'And what' they would never know as Tim was enveloped in a bear hug by a man in a chef's outfit who came running out of the restaurant, his dark eyes filled with tears.

'Isabella sent me out; she watched you arrive and guessed it was you.' He held Tim away from him. 'And you I knew in a second — you are the image of Eddie. He's not here?'

'No, I told you.' Julie couldn't take her eyes off him. 'He had to attend a conference,' she lied, unable to tell her father that Eddie had flatly refused to join them.

'Never mind, never mind, *you* are all

here. Magnificent!' He shook hands with Sam, and although he obviously wanted to envelop Julie in a bear hug, he simply kissed her on the cheek.

'Julie, I'm so happy to see you.' He brushed away a tear with the back of his hand. 'Come, come . . . forgive me . . . I'm so happy . . . and you are Jane, Sam's fiancée? Julie has told me about your engagement. We must celebrate. I have champagne on ice, you have our best table, and I cook something very special.'

* * *

He led them into the restaurant. It was spacious but every table was filled, chatter decibels were high, white-aproned waiters darted between tables carrying great bowls of pasta held at head height.

'Cool.' Tim was impressed. 'I'm starving,' he confided to his grandfather as he guided him through the room. A dark-haired girl sat behind the cash

154

desk and when she saw Carlo she stood up, smiling shyly, flanked by two small curly-haired children, a boy and a girl.

'Isabella, here they are! Angelo, Bianca — don't be shy, come and meet your English relatives.'

Julie held out her hand. Isabella looked so young, she couldn't be far off her own age. 'I'm pleased to meet you. And this is Sam, my younger brother, and his fiancée, Jane. And this is Tim, my son.'

'Yes, Carlo tells me about you so often.'

The two young children held back, hiding behind their mother.

Carlo frowned. 'Come now — they have come a long way to see you.'

'It's fine,' Julie said. 'Let them take their own time.'

Carlo suddenly clapped his hands, and the animated buzz of conversation faded. When Carlo was sure of everyone's attention he put an arm round Julie.

'Today is a wonderful day,' he

announced in Italian. 'My son and his fiancée, my daughter and my grandson have at long last come from England to visit me and my family. I hope you will all welcome them warmly to Florence so that they will return again and again. Manuel is serving drinks all round and on the house.'

Cheers, raised glasses, smiles and applause greeted the announcement. Sam looked embarrassed but Jane and Tim waved, grinning broadly.

'What's the Italian for thanks?' asked Sam.

'*Grazie*,' said Tim with a regal sort of wave.

As the cheering faded and the diners returned to their lunches, Carlo led his family to an alcove slightly apart from the main dining-room.

'My best table. Isabella and I will serve you but now I shall go back to the kitchen while you enjoy an aperitif.'

He clapped his hands and two waiters scurried over with menus and wine lists. He waved away the wine lists.

'I have chosen the wines, and I have special dishes for you, but if you see anything you would prefer on my menus just ask.'

He stood beaming at them, seemingly unable to tear himself away until, with a final pat on Tim's head, he disappeared into his kitchen.

'Please — ' Isabella smiled at them ' — sit. Children, you may sit too.' But the little ones were still too shy until Tim sat down and patted the empty chairs on either side of him. He opened the menu, pointed to some items and mimed 'What's that'?'

The little boy immediately started talking in a mixture of Italian and English. Tim caught 'pasta', 'clams', and 'chicken', and as if by magic the two boys swiftly developed Anglo/Italian communication.

'What a place,' Jane said. 'Aren't you glad we came, Sam?'

'I feel a bit overwhelmed actually. I can't much remember him.'

'Give it time,' Julie murmured. 'He's

just as I remember him — a little larger perhaps.'

The meal was memorable. Carlo produced his favourite dishes accompanied by the best Italian fine wines. The pasta was home-made, of course, and Tim pronounced that pizzas at home would never be the same again, particularly after Carlo let him put his own specially-made pizza into the wood-fired ovens in the large kitchen.

Gradually the restaurant emptied, several diners coming over to the Balboni table to wish them well and press them to return for a longer visit to their beautiful Florence.

When the last customer left, Isabella joined them for delicious sorbets and special home-made ice-cream. Finally, Carlo himself left his kitchen and joined them at their table for strong black coffee.

'Well? It was good?' He looked at them anxiously.

'Good?' Even Sam's initial prickliness had dissolved under the influence of the wonderful food and wine. 'Eddie will be green with envy when I tell him. He loves Italian food and yours in superb.'

'Good, good. So you will lunch here tomorrow and afterwards I will show you the countryside. We will take a picnic, I know just the spot.'

Angelo and Bianca left the table to stand by their father, whispering in his ear. He smiled.

'They wish you would stay with us. We have plenty of spare rooms in our apartment. We could breakfast on the terrace, there are lovely views.'

'Thank you but we're booked into a hotel and we have to leave early Monday morning. But we'd love to come for lunch — the picnic sounds great.'

Carlo nodded. 'We should have *siesta* now but that is such a waste of your little time here.'

'I think we should all like a *siesta*,' Julie said on a laugh, 'but Tim wants to do a bit more sightseeing. So, thank you so much for the incredible meal and we shall see you again tomorrow.'

Carlo's face fell but Julie felt that after the high octane welcome, they could all do with some space. It was odd seeing her father in such a totally different setting with another family, a young and beautiful wife who obviously adored him, as did his children. The little girl was already dozing against his shoulder. Carlo had a life far removed from chilly Hemsdale, a life where he was someone, where he fitted perfectly. It was ironic that she had done the same thing herself as a young girl, following her husband to America to a lifestyle where she had never quite felt easy. Just as Hemsdale suited her, so Florence suited her father.

'Can you come back later, perhaps in the evening?' Isabella pleaded.

'We'll see.' Julie felt that a compromise was best. 'But we will definitely see you tomorrow. We'll all look forward to that.'

Carlo saw them out of the now-quiet restaurant.

'I close for a while now, but open in the evening when the streets will be thronged by tourists. Now most Italians will be enjoying siesta time.'

'Very civilised.' Jane tucked her arm in Sam's. 'But as we're only here for a short while we'll probably join the visitors.' She reached up and kissed Carlo on the cheek. 'Thank you so much for welcoming me. I love it here.'

He flushed with pleasure. 'Good! You will soon be a Balboni too.'

The unspoken question about the wedding hung in the air. Sam shook his father's hand briskly, pre-empting the Mediterranean-style exchange of hugs and kisses.

'Bye for now . . . er . . . bye.'

Jane exchanged glances with Julie, both sensing that Sam was having difficulty referring to Carlo as Father or, even more difficult, Dad.

Tim had no such inhibitions. '*Ciao*, Grandpa Carlo.' He hugged his grandad, then Isabella. '*Arrivederci*,' he said to Angelo and Bianca.

Isabella flushed with pleasure and Carlo looked as though he'd won the lottery.

It was late afternoon when they left. Tim wanted to take a trip to the Leaning Tower of Pisa, about 50 miles away, but the others vetoed it.

'It's too far when we have such a limited time,' Sam said. 'Let's just wander.'

'I'd like to shop,' Jane said. 'There are lots of arcades.'

Sam pulled a face. 'Tell you what, Tim, let's you and I take a ride in a water taxi just now, while the girls go shopping. I'll hire a car in the morning and we'll go to Pisa really early and be back for lunch with . . . with . . . '

'Grandpa.' Tim was firm.

★ ★ ★

Back at their hotel at the end of the day they all decided on an early night. After the day's adventures, Tim could hardly keep his eyes open.

'I do like it though,' he murmured sleepily. 'Grandpa says I'm a quarter Italian. I'd never thought of that before. Can we come again, Mum?'

'I don't see why not.' Julie stroke his hair and smiled over at her brother. 'Are you happy you've made this trip, Sam?'

'Sort of. It's a bit . . . unsettling. I wish Eddie had come.'

'He may, in time,' said Jane.

★ ★ ★

They booked an early morning alarm but it seemed to Julie that her head had only just touched the pillow when a phone ringing roused her out of sleep.

'What ..?' She struggled to open her eyes. The luminous dial of her watch showed 3.30 a.m. She fumbled for her mobile phone. 'Hello?'

'Julie!' It was Olivia's voice, high with panic. 'Thank goodness.'

'What's happened?' Julie, now thoroughly awake, switched on her bedside light. Tim, in the twin bed across the room, stirred, sighed and turned over.

'What's wrong?' Julie kept her voice low.

'I don't know. I'm bleeding. I've got terrible pains . . . I'm scared. There's no-one here. Mike was called over to Dubai . . . I can't lose this baby . . . I can't . . . '

'Ellena?'

'I gave her the weekend off. And Mum's in London. Can you come, Julie? Please. I'm so frightened.'

'Calm down, it's the middle of the night . . . and I'm in Florence.'

'I know, I know, but . . . '

'All right, I'll come, but you must phone the hospital right now . . . '

'It's the pain — it's awful. I've tried to contact Rob but he's not answering. I wish you were here.' Olivia sounded sad and lonely.

'I *will* come as soon as I can,' Julie assured her, 'but you must phone the hospital. They'll come for you, don't drive yourself. Try not to worry — it's probably just a blip. Phone St Clements now.'

Julie dressed quickly and went down to Reception. Fortunately the duty clerk spoke good English and quickly grasped the situation. His fingers flew over the computer keyboard and ten minutes later he nodded. 'There's a flight out at seven. Heathrow eight-forty-five. Shall I take?'

'Please.'

'For one?'

'Yes.' There was no point in disrupting the others when it was most likely a false alarm.

The desk clerk asked if he could do anything else to help.

'A taxi, please, to take me to the airport.'

'Of course. Some breakfast?'

'Coffee would be great. I'll pack and let my brother know what's happening.'

Julie woke Sam, and in a whispered conference he agreed it would be best to stay on with Jane and Tim.

'It's you Olivia needs,' he said. 'She

always has to rely on you.'

'I'm sure she'll be fine. You just enjoy your day.'

'I'll move into your bed so Tim won't be alarmed when he wakes up and finds you've gone.'

'Thanks, Sam. And use the time here to get to know Dad.'

'I'll try. I'm glad we came, it was the right thing to do.'

'I think so too. I'll ring tonight.'

★ ★ ★

Julie managed to doze on the plane and phoned St Clements from Heathrow.

'This is Julie Haywood. My sister, Olivia Power, was brought in last night.'

'Oh, Julie, hi, it's Fran. Where are you?'

'Heathrow. Can you put me through to Maternity?'

'Sure. I believe Mr Kendall's with her now. He came in early. Should I page him?'

'Please. Thanks. I'll hold.'

It seemed an age before he answered: 'Hello, Julie. It's Rob Kendall.'

'Have you seen Olivia?'

'Yes, I came in with the ambulance. She's fine. It was a false alarm, but she was right to call us. She says you're in Italy. That's nice.'

'It would be if I was still there but now I'm at Heathrow.'

'You've cut your trip short? That's a shame.'

'It was only a weekend. Look, as long as Olivia's OK . . . '

'She is, really. But I'll keep an eye on her. She needs rest so we'll probably keep her in overnight. Her blood pressure's a bit high.'

'I can take her home and stay with her when I get back to Hemsdale.'

'Right. Look, I'm going home now but I could meet you at the hospital later. Ring me when you're back and I'll tell Olivia you're on your way.'

'Give her my love and — Rob, thanks.'

'All part of the service. See you soon.'

Julie's mind was more at ease after speaking to Rob. He was in charge and Olivia was OK.

She regretted missing out on the Sunday plans in Florence but she knew she would go back many times in the future. Italy had spoken to her. She was half Italian and she was going to indulge that half and make up for all the years lost.

★ ★ ★

Olivia looked lovely propped up in bed, dark hair falling over her shoulders, olive skin glowing with health, but her eyes were still fearful as Julie and Rob came to her bedside.

'Olivia, I'm so glad you're OK. Rob tells me the scan's fine and the baby's developing beautifully,' Julie said in a reassuring tone.

Tears sprang to Olivia's eyes. 'I'm so sorry for spoiling your weekend. But I was convinced I was losing the baby. Can you forgive me?'

'There's nothing to forgive. We're all at fault for going off and leaving you. We won't do it again, I promise.'

'Mike's flying home and he won't be travelling away again until the baby's born.' She took a deep breath, her smile returning. 'I just love saying that — 'when the baby's born'. And it will be fine, won't it, Rob? Rob was marvellous,' she told Julie. 'He came right away and stayed with me through the scan. Thank you so much.'

'Just doing my job — I'm glad it turned out well.'

'But your weekend . . . ?' Olivia still looked contrite.

'Forget it. We all had a wonderful day on Saturday. Florence was amazing. Tim's taken to Italy, and especially to his grandfather. He's suddenly realised he's a quarter Italian and he thinks that's so 'cool'!'

There was a long pause.

'We had lunch at Dad's restaurant,' Julie went on. 'It was great. Isabella's very pretty and Angelo and Bianca are sweet children. They're a happy family.'

Olivia turned her face away. 'I don't know how you can after what he did to us. I'm surprised at Sam, too, but I expect that's Jane's doing.'

'No. Sam found it difficult at first but I think he's coming round.'

'What about Mum? She must be upset.'

'No. Truly. Haven't you talked to her lately? She's fine about it. She's picking up new threads of her own, which is good. That's why she isn't here this weekend.'

'I know. I spoke to her earlier. Some bridge thing. She's coming in later.'

'I'm sorry to interrupt,' Rob broke in, 'but you should get some rest now, Olivia, especially if your mother's coming in later. You must be shattered too, Julie.'

'Not really, I slept on the plane. Does Mum know you're OK?'

'Yes. Will you say sorry to Sam and Jane for breaking up their weekend? Tim, too.'

'They were having such a good time, they'll hardly notice I've left! Take care and sleep well tonight.'

'I will. Rob, I feel so safe when you're around. You're not going off anywhere, I hope?'

'Not that I know of. I'm too busy settling in at St Clements.'

'I do hope you'll stay.'

'I've no plans to leave. Now — rest. The nurse will monitor you through the night and I'll look in in the morning.'

In the corridor, Rob took a firm grasp of Julie's elbow and steered her towards the hospital entrance. She tried to pull away but he tightened his grip.

'You're coming with me. I think you owe me an explanation, Mrs Haywood.'

He didn't release her until they reached his car where he handed her into the passenger seat. He got into the driving seat and started it up.

'What are you doing? I need to go home and change. I must look a wreck.'

He glanced at her briefly. 'No, you don't. You look stunning.'

171

'But where . . . ?'

'I don't know yet, just away from Hemsdale. I'm abducting you, Julie Balboni/Haywood and I'm not returning you until you tell me exactly what's bugging you about me. Got that?'

She sank down a little in her seat. 'Do I have an option?'

'Nope.'

Julie Reveals the Truth

For a while Rob drove in silence, glancing occasionally at Julie who kept her eyes half closed against the dazzle of the evening sun, now low in the sky. Without taking his eyes off the road, he adjusted her passenger seat visor.

'Is that better?'

Julie nodded, her mind racing to work out a strategy to deal with his inevitable questions. She *had* shown her anger and she knew it was ridiculous for an adult woman to harbour such a resentment from long ago. If only Rob hadn't turned up at St Clements. And yet . . . she pushed the thought away, settled further down into her seat and closed her eyes.

'Tired?' Rob asked.

'A bit. I dozed on the plane but I was too worried about Olivia to sleep properly.'

'Have you always played the 'big sister' role even though you're so much younger?'

'I suppose so. Olivia's always been the volatile one in the family — Italian temperament inherited from our father probably.'

'So you're the steady one?'

'I can't answer that — probably boring would be best.'

'I don't think you're boring.'

'You don't really know me. Where are we going?'

'You'll see. I know a place for good pub food, so I hope you're hungry.'

She sat up. 'I am, now you mention it. I had a roll on the plane and lots of coffee.'

She leaned back again, closed her eyes and thought again about how she could deal with his questions. He wasn't a fool, he'd guessed there was something, and now she felt like a complete idiot about an incident she hadn't thought about for years and which had become such an issue.

Perhaps it would be best to blurt it out and be done with it — exorcise the memory and establish a good working relationship with him.

She looked at him, relaxed and easy behind the wheel, a slight smile on his face. For a second his eyes met hers and there was a flash of intensity in the gaze. Hastily she looked away towards the lush green fields patterned with the lengthening shadows of a potentially beautiful sunset. It was a peaceful, relaxing scene. Her eyelids drooped and in a few minutes she was fast asleep.

When the car stopped Julie awoke with a start and for a brief second she thought she was in Italy. Then she remembered — she was back in England with Rob and it was show-down time.

'Where are we?'

'About twenty miles west of Hemsdale. The Shepherd's Crook Inn here is a favourite staging post for walkers.'

'What a lovely building. I imagine it's quite old,' she observed.

'It dates back originally to the twelfth century, when it started out as a shepherd's bothy. The owners try to keep the rustic touch. There are great views from the garden. I hope we can get a table outside.'

Julie followed him across a courtyard to a low stone-built building. He had to duck to avoid the low doorway beam. It was quite busy inside but the pretty middle-aged woman behind the bar greeted Rob warmly.

'Robert Kendall, you've taken your time coming out to see us. I heard you were back in this country. How are you?'

He leaned over the counter and gave her a kiss. 'All the better for seeing you, Martha. How's Jim?'

'Fine.' She glanced curiously at Julie. 'Julie Haywood,' he introduced, then, 'Martha Pilling — she and Jim have been friends of mine since I could legally be in a pub.'

Martha gave Julie a warm, wide smile. 'He practically lived here at one point. He was a regular walker, used to bring his friends from university here, and then afterwards, with Glynis . . .' She stopped and frowned. 'Rob, I'm really sorry — my big mouth. Sorry.' She changed the subject hastily. 'Can I get you a drink? I hope you're staying for a meal. Uh, Rob, I'm so sorry that . . .'

'Martha, don't worry. Please, it's all right, I'm OK now, it's been a while. Julie's a colleague and I've been telling her about your garden. Could we eat outside? It's such a fine evening.'

'Surely.' She handed them menus and smiled at Julie with perhaps a hint of disappointment at the 'colleague'.

She led them through the bar to a large garden set with tables, chairs and umbrellas. At the end of the lawned area there was an orchard where a few tables were screened by trelliswork. A fine display of climbing plants included roses and clematis, giving a fragrant privacy to the tables.

'Lucky weather,' she commented as

she fussed with knives, forks and napkins. 'It was a wash-out last weekend, terrible rainstorms. I'll send Nicky to take your order and I'll see you later.'

'What an amazing place.' Julie inhaled the perfume of the flowers. 'It's quite an enchanted bower here.'

'I thought you'd like it. When my parents moved to London I was in my last year at school. I lodged with some friends but I used to come here walking a lot at weekends. Martha and Jim set up a sort of study/bedroom in one of the outhouses. Friends would come down and we'd walk the Dales, maybe camp out, so you see why I've a soft spot for the Shepherd's Crook and its owners.'

'I can. Your parents are still in London?'

'Retired. To Seaford, near Brighton.'

'So where's your home?'

'Hemsdale, of course. You saw where I live.'

'But that's not permanent.'

'No, but I'm looking for somewhere permanent and your brother-in-law, Mike, is helping — he has lots of contacts. Don't forget, I was born and bred in Hemsdale and lived here until I went to med. school.'

'Where was that?' Julie asked, desperately avoiding the main issue.

'Nottingham.' He looked amused. 'Would you like a copy of my CV?'

'Sorry. No, it's just . . .'

A young girl approached their table with a basket of bread.

'Hello, I'm Nicky. Can I take your order? Martha says drinks are on the house — lovely New Zealand white wine.'

Rob shook his head. 'Not for me, thanks, just a half of shandy, I'm driving. Julie?'

'Sounds good. Thanks.'

'I'll bring the bottle. You can take home what's left.'

'Goodness!'

'Martha's gimmick.' Nicky grinned. 'It stops customers gulping down too much and getting arrested on the way home.'

She took their order, whisked away the menus and trotted back across the lawn.

Rob leaned his elbows on the table. 'How was Florence?'

'How did you know?'

'Olivia told me all about it.'

'Of course. Yes, it was great.'

'It's a lovely city. I've been there once. I'd like to visit again one day.'

He seemed in no hurry to address the main issue and Julie felt a stir of anger. She wanted to get it over with.

'Rob, why have you brought me here?' she asked abruptly.

'I told you, you have something against me. I've no idea what I've done but I thought a relaxed, charming spot like this well away from the hospital or Maldon's was the right atmosphere to resolve whatever it is that's worrying you..' He looked at her seriously. 'What is it, Julie? Something's definitely wrong. Sometimes you look at me with what seems to be hate in your eyes. I can't work with that.'

'I know. I'm sorry. I feel stupid and you've been so great with Olivia . . . '

'That's my job and nothing to do with this . . . whatever it is.'

'Well . . . er . . . '

'Here's the wine and your shandy,' Nicky broke in cheerfully. 'Martha says red is best with the casserole but this,' she held up the bottle, 'is just perfect, goes with the evening balmy air, birdsong, stars out later — so romantic.' She poured the wine into Julie's glass then pressed the cork back in the neck of the bottle. 'Enjoy it. See you later.'

Julie looked at Rob. He was laughing; he'd caught Nicky's cheerful mood and Julie felt so foolish that she wanted to run out of the garden, hitch a ride home and black out that silly incident so many years ago.

'Come on, Julie, there is something, isn't there? Even that first evening when I met with you and Tim, you hid your face then, and in the pub those dark glasses . . . '

Julie took a deep breath.

'OK, when I was at Fletcher I had the most terrible crush on one of the most popular, best-looking guys in the school. I was thirteen, our dad had just left us for a young Italian girl, Mum fell into deep depression, Olivia had a miscarriage — total chaos. My . . . crush . . . kept me from thinking of all that was happening at home.'

'But . . . so what's the problem with that? Fairly normal I'd say. Was it someone in your year? Would I know him?'

'You would. School captain, senior prefect, destined for glory somewhere . . . '

Rob shook his head. 'I can't see what this has to do with me.'

'It *was* you, you chump! I had a violent adolescent passion — for you.'

In the stunned silence, she felt bubbles of laughter rising in her throat; Rob looked so puzzled, so at a loss, so taken aback it was comical. He took a swig of shandy, but it went down the wrong way, and he coughed and spluttered so much that she thought he was in danger of choking.

He managed to regain control of his breathing, enough to gasp out, 'I'm flattered but what are you so angry about? It wasn't my fault!'

'It's what you said about me, that's what was so hurtful, and for some reason, whenever I look at you now I hear those words again.'

'What words? How was I to know you had a . . . a crush on me? I had a passion for your sister when I was fourteen — most of my class did, but I don't hate Olivia because she was hardly aware of me.'

'She probably didn't humiliate you.'

'Julie, I didn't even *know* you.'

Next second, she burst out, ' 'That funny-looking skinny kid with braces on her teeth? She's got a nerve! And her skin's like a volcanic eruption',' she quoted.

There, it was out. She looked at him and his eyes were angry.

'That's what it's about? A remark — which, incidentally, I'm certain I never made — years ago, that's festered to the extent that you'd let it interfere with your job? I can't believe it.'

'It haunted me for a long time. But eventually I forgot and then when I saw you at the conference, all the hurt came back. I couldn't stop it. I know it sounds stupid now, trivial . . . '

'No, it was cruel, but I never said it. I wouldn't be so . . . so callous.'

'But you did. Amanda reported it word for word. She even wrote it down.'

'Who's Amanda?'

'Amanda Burton, my friend. She said she'd fix it.'

'Fix what?'

'I don't know, I never asked.'

'Some friend! Amanda Burton — was she in your year?'

'No, the one above.'

He rubbed his eyes. 'Hang on, your friend told you I'd said that ridiculous thing? What did you do then?'

'I . . . I avoided you. I had to take time off for a while anyway to look after my mother.'

'But you believed her, this Amanda . . . ?' His eyes narrowed. 'Amanda — red hair, quite tall, looked a lot older than thirteen or fourteen? I do remember her; she used to hang around; she was always following me until I told her to get lost. Do you still know her?'

'No, she left soon after, then you left, and after a while I forgot — or thought I did — until the conference. I'm sorry, Rob, I wish to goodness I'd never mentioned it.'

'I'm glad you did, and I'm glad to set the record straight. The Amanda girl was using you for some twisted purpose. Forget it. Here's Nicky, so let's enjoy our meal.'

The two of them picked at their food but the enchanted evening had slipped away and there was just the gathering dusk.

'I can't believe I've been such an

idiot.' Julie was hot with embarrassment.

'I said, forget it.' He picked up her hand. 'It's past. It's the present and the future that count. We work together and can be friends, can't we?' He hesitated, aware of her discomfort. 'Maybe you'll come out with me again? Sort of clean slate?'

'I . . . I'm not sure. Tim's going to America in a couple of weeks and I need to spend time with him.'

'I'm sure he could let you off for one evening. Is he staying with your . . . um . . . ?'

'Geoff, his dad. Yes.'

'Are you going too?'

'No. Isn't this wonderful food?' She changed the subject abruptly.

'What I would term proper food. Yes.'

They ate in silence, no longer at ease with each other. Julie's thoughts were still running over her stupid misjudgment and its effects on her life — the way she'd rushed into marrying Geoff too young, then the predictable divorce,

Tim's one-parent family. She needed space to think.

'I should be getting back, I'm quite tired.' She pushed her plate away. 'Please tell Martha it was lovely, I'm just not very hungry. I'll see you by the car.'

★ ★ ★

Julie was far too busy in the following weeks to indulge in too much thinking. Work claimed much of her time. Teresa had suddenly left the firm for the bright lights of London and until she was replaced Julie had to monitor the work on S.A.D. as well as the new trials. Tim would soon be leaving for the States — after his final week at primary school — and she wanted to spend as much time with him as possible.

Sandra was now out a lot and while she was always happy to look after Tim, she had a calendar of things to do before she and Bee left for their weeks in France.

She had been interested in the Florence trip and seemed genuinely pleased that Carlo was a happy family man with a successful business.

'It's good, Julie — I'm beginning to enjoy life at last. I should have done it years ago. I think Bee and I might splash out on a European tour, maybe take in Florence.'

'So you should. You might even find a new man on your travels.'

Her mother laughed comfortably. 'I don't think so, dear. I'm too long in the tooth and I'm having too good a time to have to worry about a new man. You can talk anyway — talk about all work and no play. You practically live at Maldon's.'

'I know, but I'm on top of it and I can take it easy once Tim's with Geoff.'

'I thought Geoff looked very well this time, and you looked to be very good friends. I've always had a very soft spot for him.'

'Mother, stop it! Geoff and I are past

history. We have to get along for Tim's sake.'

'Mmm. How are the celebration plans for Maldon's anniversary coming along?'

'They're not. Eric keeps changing the game plan; one moment it's a posh dinner dance at one of the county's finest hotels with bed and breakfast thrown in, next it's a sort of bangers-and-mash at Maldon's HQ with a firework display.'

'Surely he'd be better off giving you all a bonus?'

'We're getting that as well, based on service, of course. I don't mind which the board chooses, just as long as they make a decision soon.'

Maldon's directors finally did make a decision. There was to be a dinner, dance and disco just for staff and partners at the Five Stars, Hemsdale's main hotel, and a further celebration in November at Maldon's with a barbecue and firework display, all invited. The dinner dance was scheduled for the fourth Saturday in July, the week after Tim left for America.

★ ★ ★

The week before Tim was due to leave, Julie had a call from Geoff.

'Hi, Julie, everything OK?'

'Yep. Tim's getting really excited. I'm driving him to Heathrow on Thursday. He's having a chaperone on the flight.'

'He won't like that, will he?' There was a pause. 'Listen, why don't you come too? I'm in the new house and it's fabulous — right beside some wonderful beaches. How about it?'

'You know I can't. I'm up to my eyes in work in any case, and besides, it's Maldon's big party the Saturday after Tim leaves.'

'Surely a trip to San Diego would be more fun than some company beano?'

'Very likely, but Maldon's is my work place. I like it and want to be at the party.'

'Come later then, even for a few days.

I'll pay your fare. I'd love to show you California.'

Julie sighed in exasperation. Same old problem — drop everything and come away with me. It had been the same when they were married and she'd just started her nursing training. She'd had to drop it and follow Geoff to America. Even there, she'd wanted to work, but Geoff had mapped out another route for her.

'No, Geoff,' she said now. 'I appreciate your offer but no, thanks.'

'I can't persuade . . . '

'No. Please, Geoff, just no.'

'OK, some other time. Love to Tim, tell him I can't wait to see him.'

'I will. Have a great time.'

Julie put the phone down. What was her ex-husband up to? Was he just between girls or was he genuinely trying to turn into a family man? The fact that he loved Tim was indisputable and she'd never denied him access. What more did he want?'

She concentrated on Tim, buying

him new gear for his trip and looking up travel information about California with him on the Internet.

On the night before his flight Tim came into her room when she was in bed. It was quite late.

'What's up, Tim, can't you sleep?'

'No, I'm fine. I just . . . um . . . I came to say that I'll miss you — and Granny. But you especially. And thanks for letting me go.'

'Oh, Tim, love.' She hugged him to her, tears pricking the back of her eyes. 'I wouldn't dream of stopping you. You'll have a fabulous time but don't forget to send me lots of post cards, e-mail, phone . . . '

'Yes, yes. You'll be OK, won't you?'

'Of course. I've got lots to do.'

'Mmm . . . Do . . . do you think . . . maybe you and Dad . . . you like him, don't you? And he likes you, he told me.'

'Tim, you mustn't think of it,' she said firmly. 'We're divorced, we're friends, and we both love you. I'm sorry but that's all there is. Sorry.'

'OK. Just asking. No worries.' He put his arms round her and gave her a kiss. 'I'll be back soon.' Then with a whoop he leapt in the air. 'And Las Vegas, here I come.'

'Las Vegas?'

'In Nevada, that's what Dad said, and the Grand Canyon.'

He came to sit on her bed and Julie knew it would be some time before he got to sleep that night.

'OK, tell me all about it.'

★　★　★

She drove home from Heathrow in a subdued mood. It had been hard to say goodbye to Tim but his chaperone was a motherly sort of woman who'd chatted to them both until his flight was called, and when they'd gone through to the departure lounge he'd waved goodbye until she could no longer see him.

Over the weekend she checked on

Olivia who was in euphoric mood.

'I'm fine. Why don't you come over here for a change for Sunday lunch? Mike and I are taking the dogs for a long walk. Do come, Julie. I saw Rob Kendall yesterday; he's really pleased with me, everything's going to plan.'

'Good. OK, I'd like to come over. It's very quiet here as you can imagine without Tim. No Sunday lunch planned here, of course.'

'Mum away again? Whatever is she up to?'

'Nothing mysterious, just enjoying life at last.'

'Good for her. See you later then.'

★　★　★

Times were changing, Julie thought as she got ready to go to Olivia's; both Tim and Sandra more independent, and Olivia on an even keel. She felt rather redundant, suddenly. Perhaps she should get out more. For some reason Robert Kendall came into her thoughts. She hadn't heard from him since the evening at Shepherd's Crook.

On impulse she phoned his mobile.

'Julie, how are you? I've been meaning to ring you.'

'Rob, I've been thinking about the other evening. I'm sorry I spoilt it and I'd like to make amends, since we have to work together.'

'You don't need to, but we could meet up for a drink — chat about the drug trials. There are one or two things . . . '

'No — I didn't mean that. Do you know there's an anniversary party at the Five Stars for Maldon's staff only? The autumn barbecue is for clients and the whole world so you'll be invited as well, but would you . . . er . . . like to come with me to the dinner and disco on Saturday?'

There was such a long silence that she began to regret the impulse.

'If you're busy, it doesn't matter,' she said quickly. 'I can ask Dan . . . '

'No, no, please, I'd love to come. I

was just mentally rearranging my diary. I'll pick you up, shall I? What time?'

'No, I'll book a taxi and pick you up — after all, I'm the hostess.'

He laughed. 'All right. I look forward to it. Is it casual or do I need to dust off my ancient dinner jacket?'

'Smart casual. Maldon's is a pretty relaxed firm — that's why I enjoy working there so much.'

'Right. But, Julie — no shop-talk between us. Agreed?'

'No shop-talk — just fun.'

Her hands were shaking as she hung up. It had been pure impulse that had driven her to invite him to the party and now she felt a tingle of excitement. For the first time, she would meet Rob Kendall untroubled by memories of the past. She was looking forward to it.

A Magical Evening

On the morning of the party Julie went downstairs to find her mother picking up her post.

'Look, a card from Tim. My goodness, he's been to Mexico! He's bought me a poncho, he says. He's having a whale of a time, isn't he?'

'It looks like it. I had an e-mail from Geoff, too, saying how well Tim has settled into — and I quote — 'the wonderful Californian lifestyle of blue skies, sun and surf'. What's he trying to prove, Mum?'

'It's fairly obvious — that Tim's happier there. That he prefers it to grey old Hemsdale.'

'That's not true! He's looking forward to going to Fletcher in September. All his friends are here, and his family.'

'Only our part of it. Geoff's got an older brother in the States, hasn't he?'

'Yes — Graham. That's why Geoff went out there in the first place, but Graham's family are in Florida.'

'I bet they'll visit San Diego while Tim's there. Graham has a couple of sons, hasn't he? Tim's cousins.'

'Yes, but they're older than Tim.'

'Don't look so worried! Geoff's doing the right thing, spending time with his son. Now, stay and have breakfast with me and tell me what you're going to wear tonight. I'll make us bacon and scrambled eggs.'

'A leisurely Saturday morning breakfast — sounds great! It's nice to have you at home this weekend. No jolly jaunts with Bee?'

'I'm going over to see her later, planning our French trip. I'm really looking forward to that.'

'I hope you'll be here for Sam's wedding,' Julie said, cracking eggs into a bowl.

'Of course I will. They haven't fixed a day yet?'

'I don't think so. It's getting pushed

back a bit, I think. Jane's parents are busy in the autumn.'

'I'm certainly not going to miss Sam's wedding, even if I have to fly back from somewhere for it!'

'You're turning into a real gadabout.' Julie paused and then took the plunge. 'Er . . . have you thought about inviting Dad to the wedding?'

Sandra paused in the middle of making coffee. 'I think that's entirely up to Sam and Jane, but do you know, I shan't mind one way or the other. In fact, I'd be quite pleased to see Carlo — and you can't imagine how happy I am to hear myself saying that.'

'Oh, Mum, I am glad.' She gave her a hug. 'I do admire you — you've been brilliant.'

'No, you're the one to admire, the way you've supported us all, then coped with a divorce and forged a career. I should have woken up years ago, but I'm very proud of you, dear.'

'Oh, Mum, don't, you'll make me cry.'

'Don't do that, we don't want too much salt in the eggs, do we?'

Julie laughed and began to whisk the eggs.

'Right, that's the mutual admiration society wound up for the day then. I just hope Geoff's not going to unsettle Tim.'

Sandra gave her daughter a shrewd look. She had her own idea about what Geoff was up to.

'It'll be all right. Now, what are you going to wear this evening?'

★ ★ ★

Julie, with her resolve 'to get out more', had splashed out on a new outfit. She took time and care with hair and make-up, and at half-past six that evening, she presented herself to Sandra for inspection.

Her mother took in the picture. Julie had picked the perfect style for her slender figure, a dark-blue chiffon dress which flared out below the hips to mid-calf length, complementing her slim ankles to perfection. Her hair fell in thick waves. Long golden earrings, sapphire studded, added elegance to the whole ensemble.

'Well!' Sandra exclaimed. 'Quite lovely. What a beautiful dress.'

'What about the shoes? They're a bit higher than I usually wear.' Strappy sandals with diamante trim added extra inches to her height. 'I hope I don't fall over. They were a bit of a silly buy really. It's an age since I wore anything but flats or trainers. I'm not over-dressed, am I?'

'Not a bit, it's all lovely. Are you going to bring Rob back for coffee?'

'We'll see how it goes. I've ordered a taxi.'

'*You've* ordered a taxi?'

'Don't look so shocked, Mum, that's what independent women do.'

'Hmm.' There was a ring at the door. 'That'll be it now, I expect.'

Julie walked carefully down the drive to the taxi, gingerly testing the new shoes.

The taxi picked up Rob ten minutes later. He slid into the seat next to her and kissed her on the cheek. 'Right on time — and you look lovely.'

'Thanks. My shoes are a bit of a problem. I should have practised!'

'You'll be fine. Take them off if they hurt.'

Rob was wearing light-coloured trousers, a dark silk jacket and an open-neck white shirt. 'I've bought a tie, just in case I need it.' He patted his pocket. 'One of the good things about where we were in Ghana, there was no dress code, anything went.'

'Do you miss it?'

'It's taking a while to settle back here. Obviously it's a different world. Values are so different, and as for medicine, if they had a tenth of the resources we have . . . ' He paused, looking sheepish. 'Stop me before I jump on to my hobby horse.'

'No, it's interesting.'

'No, tonight's a party night — so let's party.'

'Five Stars,' the taxi driver announced, and they climbed out.

Rob took her arm. 'This is a novel experience, being taken out by a young woman.'

'Really?' Julie longed to ask more and maybe find out about the mysterious Glynis, but this was neither the time nor the place.

The hotel foyer was crowded with guests, with waitresses circulating with champagne, and a dinner-jacketed manager attempting to filter everyone through into the ballroom.

'I thought you said smart casual?' said Rob. 'I can see lots of dinner jackets.'

'Those are the bosses, directors, top nobs. Lots of people are tie-less — look, there's a guy over there in some sort of jumper thing.'

Rob took a couple of glasses of champagne from a passing waitress, handed one to Julie and guided her to an alcove just by the ballroom.

'Julie, I have to say this. I'll never

refer to it again, but that picture — the one Amanda or whatever she was called, painted of me — was pure fantasy. You could never have looked like that, or if you did, you have a fairy godmother who transformed you into a beautiful woman.'

She felt a surge of happiness at his words and smiled as she raised her glass. 'Thank you — but I did wear braces on my teeth for a while and I did have a few spots. And I can say now that you were an extremely attractive young man . . . boy? You seemed terribly old to me then.'

'To the future then.' They clinked glasses, drank, and Rob kissed her lightly on the lips.

'Hey, you two,' a familiar abrasive voice broke in. 'It's a bit early for that.' Polly Fellowes, glass in hand, poked Rob in the back.

'Polly,' Julie said, 'how did . . . ?'

'I was invited. My good friend Duncan here is one of Maldon's chief boffins. We practically grew up together.

Duncan, this is Rob Kendall, St Clements, and Julie you should know. She works at Maldon's.'

A tall, bespectacled, mild-looking man held out his hand.

'Julie Haywood, isn't it? I've seen you around but I think we work at opposite ends of the building. Polly makes me come to these dos, but they're not my cup of tea at all.'

'I need to keep my ear to the ground.' Polly frowned. 'Especially now I'm doing most of the work on this new drug of yours. We'll sit with you at dinner,' she decided. 'How's that good-looking husband of yours, Julie?'

'All right, as far as I know. Tim's with him in San Diego right now for the school holidays.'

'Did he stay with you at that dear little cottage when he was here?'

'He was with Tim mainly. I was working. We'll see you later — I must go and speak to Eric and his wife.'

'Do we have to sit with Polly?' Rob asked in a low voice as they broke away.

'I see quite enough of her at work.'

'We'll certainly try to avoid it. She can be a touch abrasive.'

'A touch? She's suddenly become all proprietorial over your trial, too.'

'That's strange. When I spoke to her originally, she didn't want to know.'

Rob shrugged. 'Well, she seems to be doing a good job. That's what matters.'

Eric Lancaster insisted that Rob and Julie joined their party for dinner which was a lengthy affair punctuated by a lot of speeches. Some were very good, witty and to the point, but one or two were simply meandering reminiscences by a couple of retired directors. Finally Eric stood up to launch into a last speech of the evening.

'It's nearly eleven o'clock,' Rob muttered. 'There's not a lot of time left for dancing.'

'Well, I suppose the dinner and speeches were the main events. Haven't you enjoyed it?'

'Of course — it's just that I'd like to dance with you before we have to go home at midnight.'

The thought of being held in Rob's arms made Julie's stomach clench. She was enjoying the evening more than she'd thought possible — the party atmosphere, the buzz of conversation, and above all, being easy with Rob.

There was a hush as Eric Lancaster started to speak: 'I trust we've all enjoyed the evening. I certainly . . . ' He broke off suddenly as a cluster of men appeared in the doorway, two police constables, another in plain clothes, and the manager of the Five Stars.

The manager came to Eric's side and stooped to speak quietly in his ear. 'Sorry to interrupt the festivities but the police want to speak to you.'

As Eric crossed the dining-room, there was a buzz of speculation.

'Probably illegal parking.'

'Accident?'

'Drugs raid?'

The speculations became more and more wild as the police spoke to Eric whose face grew more serious by the second. He nodded to the constables and returned to his table.

'I'm sorry, folks, something's come up at Maldon's, but there's no need to let it spoil the fun. I'm going with the police to investigate and I'll keep you informed. Enjoy the rest of your evening, and don't forget, the company has laid on coaches to take you home.'

He spoke briefly to his wife whose eyes widened. He patted her shoulder, and then left with the police.

The company, chattering more than ever, split into groups, some to the bar, others to the dance floor. Polly Fellowes came up to Rob and Julie. She looked odd, Julie thought, and there was a curious suppressed excitement in her face as she spoke. 'Any idea what's going on?'

'No. Eric didn't tell us a thing. He spoke to his wife, and she's staying here, so it can't be anything too dreadful.'

'Come and have a drink with us,' Polly suggested.

Rob frowned. 'I was hoping to have a dance with Julie.'

Duncan looked at his watch. 'I don't want to be too late, Polly. We've got family coming for Sunday lunch.'

'Oh, for goodness' sake, one drink, then I'll release you. Come on, Rob, Julie.'

They had no option but to follow Polly and her reluctant escort into the crowded bar.

'Where's Gary?' Julie whispered. 'I thought he was the current boyfriend.'

'He is, but I don't think a dinner dance is his cup of tea any more than it's poor old Duncan's. But we *will* get our dance in, Julie.'

However, it was very nearly midnight before Rob was able to take Julie on to the dance floor for the very last dance of the evening, an old-fashioned waltz. Rob was a very good dancer. He held her firmly and she melted towards him as they moved as one.

'I wish we could have danced more.' His lips touched her ear.

'Perhaps another time.'

The music stopped, the manager said a few words and the evening was over. The celebration had been a success and everyone began to talk of the barbecue and fireworks scheduled for the autumn. The other topic on everybody's lips, of course, was what had happened at Maldon's?

Julie's taxi was waiting for them, the driver listening to the radio. He switched it off as Julie and Rob appeared. 'Had a good evening?'

'Excellent. Any local news on the radio?'

'I wasn't listening. Why?'

'Oh, nothing.' Rob pulled the door to. 'Maybe there's something on the local television news. Is it too late for a cup of coffee? We can stop at my flat — it's before your house — then I can run you home. I've hardly had anything to drink.'

Julie looked at the time. It was only ten past midnight and she felt wide awake.

'Why not? Mum said to bring you back for coffee, but she'll be in bed by now. Mind you, I doubt if there'll be anything on TV about Maldon's.'

'It'll be on the Internet if there is anything.' He took Julie's hand and held it all the way back to the flat.

His apartment looked a little more lived-in than the previous time she'd been there. Two miniature pot roses gave bright splashes of colour — definitely evidence of a female influence, she thought with a stab of disappointment. A large mohair throw on the sofa added a luxury touch.

Rob came through from the kitchen. 'Coffee's on. Do you want a liqueur? Brandy? Tia Maria?'

'No, thanks, coffee will be fine. This room looks different. It's nice.'

He laughed. 'My mother's been on a visit and she dropped a few things off, bless her.' He indicated the bone china cups. 'She cleared the crockery cupboard, too — and her cast-off pans are in the kitchen. Gave her a good excuse to buy more, she said.'

'Any luck with the house-hunting?'

'Not so far. But I'm OK here for a bit. I'm hardly ever here anyway. I practically live at St Clements. I enjoyed tonight. It made a real change. How's Tim doing in California?'

'Loving it, he says, and Geoff is very enthusiastic. He's giving Tim a great time.'

'That's good.' He poured coffee into the china cups. 'You must have married very young. Tim's what — eleven?'

'Yep. I was seventeen. He was twenty-three. Mum was against it, of course. Not that she didn't like Geoff — but she thought, quite rightly, that I was far too young.'

'So why did you do it?'

She took a sip of coffee and looked him in the eye. 'You — or what I thought was you. You see . . . those remarks Amanda made knocked all the confidence out of me. I took refuge in my family, made myself indispensable. And then Geoff came along and he found me . . . *me*, attractive.'

'You are.'

'Yes, well, I didn't feel it then. Anyway, Geoff was older, confident, in love with me — it was wonderful. We married, lived in the cottage at Moorland View, and I started nursing training. Then Tim came along. I was happy, I loved the moors, I planned to carry on nursing training.'

'Then what?'

'Geoff's firm sent him to Florida. It was very swift promotion — he's a bright guy. He loved it and wanted me and Tim to join him. I didn't want to leave my family but of course I had to go. I thought I could resume my training and make a career in the States. Unfortunately Geoff thought otherwise. I was to be the corporate wife, a hostess, a stay-at-home support.

'I hated it — it was so boring and false. I missed Hemsdale, too. We started to quarrel and it all fell apart. We tried to make it work but Geoff was away a lot and the final straw was when

213

he began an affair with someone at work. I came home, worked hard at nursing, got a job at St Clements . . . and the rest you know. I couldn't have done it without my family, though. Mum was great. She practically brought Tim up. It was good for her, too, gave her a focus.'

'There hasn't been anyone else since then?'

'No. I know it's a cliché, but once bitten, twice shy. A divorce, however amicable, and ours wasn't bad, is pretty shattering. And you? You can't tell me there's been no-one in your life.'

He leaned back against the sofa, eyes closed.

'No, but it's taken me a long time to get over . . . it. Africa helped, although Africa was the cause, too.' He sighed painfully. 'You've been frank with me, so I'll tell you quickly, then I don't want to talk about it again. I fell in love there with an aid worker, Glynis. I'd never met anyone like her, her energy and dedication were amazing. We were engaged for six months, planned to marry in Ghana, work there for a few years, maybe, before coming back to Britain.'

He cleared his throat, got up and walked around the room.

'Glynis was killed in a riot. People were injured and we went to help. She was killed by a stray bullet — instantly.'

There was silence before Julie said softly, 'Oh, Rob, I'm so sorry.'

He came back to the sofa and sat down beside her. 'I blamed myself for not stopping her going out to help. Strangely, though, she always said she was destined to die in Africa. She loved it, but it killed her.

'I stayed on for a year afterwards but it wasn't the same. I had a spell in Australia, then I came home, looked around for a while, did some locum work — then I felt the pull of my roots and came back to Hemsdale.'

'I'm glad you told me.'

'It's been that sort of evening. Now, wasn't I going to check on the Internet for news about Maldon's?' He switched on his computer. 'Here we are, local Yorkshire. It *is* in the news! Look — 'Maldon's Pharmaceutical Targeted' . . . 'medical research laboratory' . . . 'fire in one of the storage rooms' . . . 'graffiti' . . . 'first warning'. That's all there is.'

Julie glanced at her watch. 'I must get home. We'll know more in the morning. Nobody was hurt, I hope? The security guard?'

'It doesn't say. Do you think it's animal rights activists? But Maldon's don't use animals for testing, do they?'

'Not that I know of.'

'But testing on animals must be done somewhere,' he pressed.

'Honestly, it's not something that's come up.' Julie slipped her jacket on. 'Thanks for coming with me tonight, Rob. I enjoyed it.'

'Thanks for asking me, it's been great. Maybe you'd come with me to The Shepherd's Crook again one evening? Martha was disappointed not to see you after the meal.'

'I'm sorry about that. Yes, I'd love to go back.'

'I'll check my calendar, and the weather forecast — we'd be lucky to have such magical weather again.'

It was a short drive through the deserted streets of Hemsdale. Julie still wasn't the least bit tired but she knew the evening had to end and was only sorry the news about Maldon's had left a jarring note.

They drew up outside her home and Rob turned her to him.

'Thanks again . . . ' He kissed her lightly, hesitated, then the kiss deepened, and Julie responded, feeling the fire of desire for the first time in years, since the early days with Geoff.

Finally they parted.

'It's late.' She sighed. 'I must go.'

He kissed her again, but briefly. 'Till next time,' he breathed.

He walked with her to the entrance to her home, waited until she found her key and quietly opened the front door.

'Goodnight, Julie.' He kissed her again with increasing passion until she broke away.

'Goodnight,' she breathed before letting herself into the silent house. For some minutes she leaned against the door, re-running the evening, trying to sort out her feelings for Rob Kendall. Then, with a sigh, she climbed the stairs, tiredness now catching up with her.

Concern About Maldon's

In Tim's absence Sandra and Julie had developed a habit of breakfasting together. On the day after the party they took longer than usual as Julie told her mother all about it.

'I didn't hear you come in; were you very late?' Sandra asked as she poured second cups of coffee.

'Not too bad. We had a coffee stop at Rob's and then he drove me back here.'

'And you enjoyed the evening?'

'Yes, it was good, a great success.' Julie paused. 'Aren't you off to France at the end of next week?'

'No need to change the subject, I'm not prying, just interested.'

'Sorry, Mum, of course you're interested. But it was just a works party. OK, I do like Rob, he's attractive and good company. I would have brought him back here but it was quite late and

219

I knew you'd be in bed.'

'You would tell me if . . . '

'I would but there's nothing to tell. Now, are you getting excited about your trip?'

'I am. We both are. We leave Friday week. I'm glad Tim's home next weekend; at least you won't be lonely.'

'No, and we'll have the family Sunday lunch next week to hear all about Tim's trip. I'm glad you'll still be here.'

'Me too. I've missed the dear boy. Oh, there's another card from him. It came yesterday.' She passed Julie a postcard, a picture of the Grand Canyon, Arizona.

'Geoff's certainly showing him all the sights,' Julie commented, turning the card over to read Tim's message. *Looking forward to seeing you all, lots to tell you AND a big surprise.* 'Hmm, wonder what that's about?'

She put the card on the dresser and turned on the kitchen TV.

'There may be something on the

news about Maldon's. Oh, look — there is! It's the national news too.'

She turned up the volume as an interviewer faced a tired-looking Eric Lancaster.

'Mr Lancaster — as Managing Director of Maldon's you must be very concerned about the attack on your premises last night. Is this the first time such a thing has happened?'

'Yes. We haven't had any problems before this. We are a medical research company concerned with monitoring trials of new drugs.'

'You carry out experiments on animals?'

'No. Maldon's haven't used animals for twenty years . . .'

'But weren't the intruders protesting against the use of animals?'

'They were misinformed. There are no animals at Maldon's.'

'But you must use animals before testing drugs on humans.'

'I repeat, there are no animals at Maldon's.'

The interviewer nodded. 'And you have no idea who might have attacked your buildings? I believe there was quite a lot of damage and a security guard was hurt?'

'The damage was minimal. We have very secure premises, although I shall still be looking at ways to increase security, and especially to protect our staff. A guard was hurt, but he was discharged from hospital this morning, thank goodness.'

'So you do expect further attacks — even after increasing security?'

'I repeat, we do not carry out animal experiments at Maldon laboratories.'

'But you don't rule out the possibility that you might be targeted again?'

'Well, of course I can't but . . . '

'Sorry, Mr Lancaster, we're out of time. Thank you for talking to us.'

Eric disappeared from the screen and the announcer went on to the next item of news. Julie switched off the TV.

'Gracious!' Sandra was wide-eyed. 'Why didn't you tell me that?'

'I really don't know anything except that the police turned up quite late in the evening at the Five Stars and spoke to Eric who left the party with them.'

'Who was responsible, do you think?'

'Goodness knows. There are lots of animal rights groups. I don't know why Maldon's should suddenly have been targeted.'

'Is it serious?'

'I don't know but it probably will be now. I think Eric was a bit foolish in making such a statement.'

'Surely not now he's denied animal testing. There'd be no point.'

'Mum, most drugs have to be tested on animals before humans. It's just not done at Maldon's.'

'Then where?'

Julie shrugged. 'Abroad, all sorts of countries, but now Eric's gone on television he's brought Maldon's into the limelight. There are two sides to issues like this — and there's lots of understandable outrage at animal experiments. I think Eric should have left it for the police to deal with, but he's the boss so it's his decision. I just hope he hasn't put Maldon's in the firing line.'

Eric must have moved very quickly over the weekend. Maldon's looked comparatively untouched on Monday morning, with a couple of boarded-up windows and a stretch of smashed chain-link fencing the only evidence of an attack. Graffiti was daubed on the walls of some of the laboratories but it was already being dealt with when the staff arrived.

'Mr Lancaster's called a meeting for all personnel,' Lucy told Julie.

Eric Lancaster's meeting was brief and to the point; staff were to be vigilant and to report anything untoward to him or to one of the directors, who would pass the information on to the police if necessary. He was sure this was just a one-off maverick piece of spite.

Later in the day he called in at Julie's office.

'Good party,' Julie said. 'Pity about the finale.'

'Indeed.' He frowned. 'The problem is that this group, or person, whoever it is, is looking specifically at our new pregnancy drug.'

'Why? How would anyone know about it?'

'I've no idea — yet. But leaflets were left in the offices and laboratories. They believe that our research is using animals . . . '

'But that's not true.'

'The truth doesn't seem to matter, I'm afraid. We're only in the early stages of clinical trials — maybe we should call a halt for a while.'

'No!' Julie cried. 'It's going so well. You can't abandon the project just because of one incident.'

'One incident could be the beginning of something more serious and I don't want to put my staff in any danger,' Eric said. 'There's a board meeting tomorrow; we'll see what emerges from that. But you're doing good work and if we have to call a halt there are plenty more projects in the pipeline.'

'This is my first baby,' Julie sighed.

'Fingers crossed then. I don't think the break-in was a collective job, more likely a one- or two-person job, and Maldon's is a strange target. We're a comparatively small arm of the bigger company and I've deliberately kept a low profile here.'

* * *

The following week passed without incident. Police and forensic personnel visited Maldon's and talked to staff but they were no further forward with their enquiries as to who was responsible for the attack. Julie looked forward to the weekend for Tim's homecoming and she and her mother were busy organising a welcome-home party.

Tim's plane was due at Heathrow on Friday evening and Julie planned to leave work at mid-day to pick him up, but as she cleared her e-mails on

Thursday she received one from Geoff telling her there was a change of plan — Tim would be arriving at Leeds/Bradford airport early on Saturday morning.

She was relieved to escape a Friday afternoon drive to Heathrow during the worst of the traffic but was puzzled by the change.

There was a light mist when she set off early on Saturday, showing signs of an early autumn. Sandra had toyed with the idea of coming with her but had opted instead to make preparations for a good British fry-up breakfast, a great favourite of Tim's.

As Julie reached the airport a hazy sun was struggling to push aside the mist and her excitement was rising at the thought of seeing her son again. She'd missed him and would be delighted to have him back.

The plane was on time and as she made her way to Arrivals, passengers were already beginning to trickle in. Eagerly she scanned the passengers.

It seemed an age before she saw Tim, who was frantically waving, and for a second she hardly recognised him. He was dressed in shorts and a T-shirt, patterned with a large picture of a surfer. His hair was quite blond, he was deeply tanned and he appeared to have grown at least a couple of inches.

'Hi, Mum!' He hugged her tightly. 'I've had a great time. Look, I've got presents. How's Granny? How are you? Have you missed me?'

'Oh, Tim, love, I certainly have, we all have. It's so good to see you.' She held him away from her. 'You look . . . different. You've grown and you're so tanned — and your hair . . .'

'It's a fantastic climate, Mum. You should go there.'

'Where's your chaperone? You didn't fly on your own, did you?'

'No, that's the big surprise. I didn't need a chaperone — look . . .'

'Hi, Julie. Surprise . . .'

'Geoff!'

'I wangled a business trip to Leeds,

juggled the flights, and here we are. Tim's had a great time and we've all loved him.'

'Who's we?'

'Oh, all the guys he met up with, and Graham and his family came over from Florida for a week and we all went game fishing.'

'And we caught lots of fish,' Tim broke in excitedly, 'and we had a party . . . and a barbecue . . . and . . . '

'But . . . ?'

'Don't look so baffled, Julie, it's quite straightforward.' Geoff laughed at her confusion. 'I've a job to do in Leeds, so I'm simply combining it with bringing my son home.'

Julie noted the emphasis on 'my son'. She swallowed. There was no alternative but to accept the situation with good grace.

'Fine.' She smiled. 'It was good of you, Geoff, and I know Tim's had a wonderful time. Where are you staying?'

'Well, I thought I could come home with you today, maybe stay over. Tim says there's a family welcome party at Loughrigg, I'd like to see everyone again. You don't mind, do you?'

'We-ell — no. No, of course I don't. I'm just surprised, that's all.'

'Dad can have my room, Mum.'

'No need. Gran's got spare rooms. She'll be pleased to see you, Geoff.'

She might as well make the best of things, she told herself, but she couldn't help feeling uneasy. It was obvious Geoff was trying to edge back into her life and she wasn't sure she could handle it.

Sandra was indeed pleased to see Geoff, as was the rest of the family. At the Sunday barbecue he fitted smoothly back in.

* * *

It was a strange weekend for Julie and she was glad to be back at work on Monday — at least she knew where she stood there. Teresa's replacement started that morning and Julie's first task was to brief her on the S.A.D. project.

The girl, Judy, was a quick learner and soon grasped the main essentials. She took over the files and promised to get back to Julie if there were any problems.

'I hope you'll be happy here,' Julie said. 'Maldon's is a good firm to work for.'

'There's been trouble though, hasn't there? Animal rights activists? It's a bit of a worry, My husband wasn't too keen on me working here.'

'I'm sure it'll be fine,' Julie said, more reassuringly than she felt.

When Rob phoned in the late afternoon, her heart gave a little lurch. She hadn't heard from him since the anniversary celebration.

'Julie, I'm sorry I haven't called before. I had to go to Seaford; my dad was taken ill.'

'I'm sorry to hear that. I hope it's not serious?'

'Heart attack. Mum was in a bit of a

state, and I felt I had to stay. Things look OK now though. Julie, I want to thank you for asking me to the party, I had a great time.'

'I enjoyed it too. You've heard about the break-in?'

'Yes, any news on it?'

'No. Eric's tightened up security here, though we're hoping it was a one-off.'

'Let's hope so. What I really phoned for is to ask if you'd like to pay a return visit to the Shepherd's Crook one evening this week?'

'This week?' Her thoughts whirled. 'I'm not sure . . . Geoff's here. He brought Tim back with him. I didn't expect him, but it's a business trip.'

There was a pause.

'I see,' said Rob. 'Well, you'll be busy then. How long is he staying?'

'I've no idea. I didn't expect him at all.'

'But that's good isn't it — for Tim?'

'Yes . . . but . . . '

'Don't worry. I'll be in touch. The

trials are going well, by the way; Polly's working hard on them. See you soon,' and he rang off.

'Drat it!' Julie banged her fist on her forehead. Why had she mentioned Geoff? Rob's voice had cooled at once. She picked up the phone to call him back, but then stopped. Better to contact him after Geoff had left again, or at least once she knew what his plans were.

★ ★ ★

Geoff returned from Leeds that evening and Sandra cooked supper for them all. He was full of news about his company and the day in Leeds had gone well.

'There's a lot of business here in the north,' he said. 'I hadn't realised the potential. Sandra, this is great food! It's a while since I had such a roast dinner. Yorkshire pudding too.'

Sandra looked pleased. 'Don't you cook? You should look after yourself.'

'I'm fine. There are good restaurants

233

right where I live, aren't there, Tim? Remember that lobster place?'

'Ace!' Tim rolled his eyes. 'But your cooking's great, too, Granny.'

Julie could see her mother was enjoying the family atmosphere.

'How long are you staying, Geoff?' Sandra asked.

'Well, I'm pretty flexible. I'd like to pop down to the cottage while the weather's still good, and if I work it right I can be around when Tim starts at his new school. I'd like to make sure it's . . . um . . . suitable.'

'It's perfectly suitable.' Julie's hackles rose. 'We should know — all of us went there. And Tim's visited it. It's a good school. Tim will be happy, all his friends are there.'

'Sorry.' Geoff held up his hands. 'I didn't mean to interfere. Can I help clear up, Sandra?'

'Gracious, no! You've had a busy day, I'm sure. Why don't the three of you go out for a walk? It's a lovely evening.'

'I'm going round to Liam's,' Tim

said. 'Mum and Dad can go though.'

'No, thanks,' Julie said hastily, 'I've work to do.'

'Come out for a drink later then,' Geoff said.

'Maybe,' she temporised. She *should* have a talk with him; it was getting far too cosy, which was unsettling for Tim.

'Yes, all right then, give me an hour or so. And, Tim, don't be too long at Liam's — it's quite late already.'

'Aw, Mum, it's still the holidays for another week. I went to bed much later in San Diego; one night we stayed on the beach until well after midnight, surfing by moonlight.'

'Did you? Well, there's not a lot of opportunity for that in Hemsdale. And you should be getting to bed earlier, ready for starting school next week.'

'Aw . . .'

'Best to do what your mother says,' Geoff put in.

'OK, Dad. Just an hour at Liam's, then I'll be back.'

'Good lad.' Geoff smiled.

Julie went up to her flat, opened up her laptop, stared at the blank screen for several minutes, then closed it. It was difficult to concentrate; Geoff's presence in the house was unsettling. Her mother was making such a fuss of him, it was no wonder he wanted to stay on.

She went downstairs to find them in a conspiratorial huddle on the living-room sofa.

'Hi.' Geoff looked up. 'We're just going back over old times. I haven't seen some of these photos of Tim before.'

'I always send you recent copies if they're any good.'

Sandra closed the album. 'I just thought . . . '

'It's all right, Mum. Maybe Geoff and I should go out. Work can wait. I think we need to talk.'

'Great!' Geoff picked up his jacket. 'See you later, Sandra.'

'We shan't be late,' Julie put in.

They walked for a while without speaking.

'Shall we try the Feathers?' Geoff suggested.

'I don't think so — the Dalesman will be quieter.'

It *was* quiet in the Dalesman and there wasn't a soul in the Snug, off the main bar. Geoff ordered a pint for himself, Julie fruit juice.

'Look, Geoff,' she said briskly, 'I think it's wonderful of you giving Tim such a fantastic holiday, and lovely that you could bring him back, but I don't think it's a good idea for you to hang around here for too long.'

'Hang around? That doesn't sound very pleasant. Tim *is* my son.'

'I know, but it's unsettling for him, you being here. It gives him false hope.'

'*Is* it false hope?'

He leaned forward and took her hand. 'No, don't move away, I've got to say this — it's what I've come for. Can't we give it another chance, Julie? I was so wrong to let you go, we were too young and very foolish. I'm older and wiser now and I know what I want. I want you and Tim and I want us to be together as a family.' His grip tightened as she tried to pull away. 'Please, Julie.'

'Don't. I . . . I just don't know what to say, what to think . . . '

'Think how much we loved each other, think of our early years. America was a mistake. Oh, don't misunderstand me — I loved it, I still do. I want to stay there. But if it means not having you with me, maybe I'd be prepared to let it go.'

'You're not making sense. It's over — it was over years ago. You can't come back into my life, I'm happy here and . . . '

'What about Tim? He wants us to be together, you can't deny that.'

'No, I can't, but we can't go back, Geoff.'

'I'm not giving up. We get on well together, don't we?'

'But I don't love you and you don't love me.'

Now he tried to draw her nearer to him across the small pub table.

'I could, though. I did once, passionately, and I find myself thinking of you a lot.'

'What about Lyndy?'

He looked startled. 'What about her? I told you, that's over.'

'Oh, Geoff, come on, you were mad about her! You practically pushed Tim and me out of the house to make room for her.'

'You were ready to go. You couldn't wait to get back to Hemsdale.'

'True. I didn't like the life you'd mapped out for me but I would have stuck it out — for Tim's sake.'

'So why not now?'

She sighed in exasperation. 'Now's different. I'm happy, I've got a good job, friends, family . . . We were both too young. And I've been to see Dad and his new family. I want to really get to know them.'

'All right, I give in — for now. But you can't deny we get on well. I'm happy in your company.'

'And that, as I keep telling Mum, is because we're *not* married. Let's keep it that way. Now, let me buy you another drink. I'll have a glass of wine too, since it's too late for work now. Let's just chat, relax — tell me about your new job and how Graham and his family are doing.'

He smiled at her and she couldn't help smiling back. She *did* like him — it was good to see him and he'd made Tim very happy.

'Well, if you're buying, I'll have a double malt whisky.'

Her eyes widened for a second, then they both laughed.

'Why not? We'll drink to Tim's homecoming.'

'I'll drink to us,' Geoff said, 'and to the future.'

Drama!

It was agreed that Geoff should spend a few more days in Hemsdale to allow him to spend time with Tim at the cottage and also to see him into his first couple of days at secondary school. He would stay with Sandra until his flight back to California. Sandra was to start her own adventure the following day.

It all fitted, but Julie couldn't help feeling uneasy. Tim was beginning to take his dad's presence for granted, so the break, when it came, would be hard.

The beginning of September saw a weather change. Summer sunshine was chased away by rain and blustery winds, but Tim and Geoff set out for the cottage in good spirits.

'It's the last few holiday days, Tim — make the most of them.' Julie was seeing them off before she went to work.

'We've lots of plans. And you're coming on Saturday, aren't you?'

'I hope so. Don't forget to call in on Alice and Harry.'

'I won't. I've got presents for them.'

'Bye, Julie,' Geoff kissed her cheek. 'See you Saturday.'

Julie waved until the car was out of sight. Her conscience was troubled. As Tim grew up, he would need his father more than ever. But could she really leave Hemsdale and make a new life with Geoff? She didn't love him. Would a life without love be possible — for Tim's sake?

She shook her head. Once Geoff was back in California, things would settle back to normal. With a new school and new friends, Tim would soon be absorbed in his Hemsdale life once again.

★   ★   ★

There was a police car outside Maldon's when she arrived. Inside there was the usual buzz of speculation among the staff. Her secretary, Lucy, a single mother with two children, was on flexi-time and had picked up the rumours earlier.

'I think there have been some threatening calls and e-mails but Mr Lancaster's being very tight-lipped about it. I'm a bit worried. Don't these groups target staff at research laboratories? Aren't *you* worried?'

'A bit, I suppose, but there's not a lot we can do,' said Julie. 'We can't stop the work we're doing. If it hadn't been for medical research, lots of us would be dead by now. It's a difficult issue and there are strong feelings on both sides, but we can't give way to bully tactics.'

A memo was later sent to all staff telling them there had been a spate of threatening e-mails and letters from an unknown source. The police were looking into it, while the chairman continued to put out press statements denying the use of animals, inviting whoever was responsible for the attacks to identify themselves, and Eric Lancaster would personally take them on a tour of Maldon's premises to prove there were no animals involved whatsoever.

For once, by Friday evening, Julie was glad to leave work and get away from the atmosphere of suspicion and uncertainly. She began to look forward to the weekend at Moorland View.

Back home, Julie found her mother packing for her trip.

'Have a cup of tea with me. I'm not making much headway with organising myself. I've lost the holiday habit, it's been so long.' Her mother's eyes sparkled and her cheeks were flushed. 'I'm really excited.'

'So I see. There's no tea in the pot, only water.'

'Gracious, what an idiot! Oh, I forgot, Jane rang, then Olivia.'

'Olivia's OK, is she?'

'Fine. She wants you to go to supper

one night next week. I shan't be here and Geoff'll be gone. What about Tim?'

'I'll take him. He and Mike can play snooker while Olivia and I baby chat. What did Jane want?'

'The wedding's fixed for just before Christmas. They'll probably have snow. She asked me about Carlo.' There was a pause as Sandra fiddled with the tea cups. 'Do you want some shortbread, dear?'

'Yes, please. And . . . ?'

'And I said . . . I said fine, invite them all. I shan't mind a bit.'

'Oh, Mum,' Julie hugged her. 'You're great! That is so nice of you.'

'Well, Jane was keen. She seems quite taken with Carlo's family so it would be wrong not to do as she wishes. It's *her* wedding, after all, and I'm just happy that Sam's marrying a girl we all love.'

★   ★   ★

Julie set off for the Dales next day in a light-hearted mood. It was very blustery but a fitful sun scudded in and out of the piled-up clouds and the forecast was fairly good.

Tim and Geoff were looking out for her and she was struck again by the resemblance between them. Tim was always going to be a reminder of her years with Geoff.

They had a day of walking and picnics well planned. At the end of it, after supper cooked by Geoff and Tim, Tim went upstairs to watch TV.

Geoff lit the fire in the sitting-room and produced a bottle of wine.

'It's been a great weekend. I can't remember enjoying a trip back more than this one. Tim's fantastic — I wish I could spend more time with him.' He uncorked the bottle and poured wine into two glasses. 'Here's to you, Julie, and thanks — and I meant every word I said the other evening . . . I want you to come back to me.'

'Geoff, I can't, you've got to accept it. I'll always be happy to see you here and you have unlimited access to Tim.

He's obviously hooked on California, so I expect he'll spend more time with you as he gets older.'

Geoff took a sip of wine.

'Julie, is there someone else? Because if there is . . . '

A picture of Robert Kendall flashed unbidden into her mind. She screwed up her eyes. 'Um . . . no, of course not.'

He gave her a long, considering look and picked up his glass.

'I'll just check on Tim. I promised to watch the football with him.'

Julie didn't see him again before she went to bed.

During the night, the wind increased in force, howling round the two moorland cottages like a demented banshee. In the early hours of the morning, Julie suddenly woke to a loud banging outside.

She sat up in bed listening — there it was again, even louder, followed by a shout, then a cry.

Jumping out of bed, she went to the window. The area was in blackness except for a light bobbing away from the Lunns' cottage. Almost immediately the Lunns' cottage lights blazed on and a figure came running out of the door. With the light streaming behind her, Julie made out Alice's figure. She was shouting and waving her arms.

Pulling on a coat, Julie thrust her feet into shoes and raced downstairs, calling for Geoff as she ran. Opening the front door she saw Alice coming towards her, overcoat over her nightdress.

'Oh Julie, help! It's Harry. They've knocked him out. There's blood . . . please come . . . '

Geoff came downstairs, yawning. 'What . . . ?'

Julie glanced at him quickly. 'Harry's hurt.' She turned back to Alice. 'We're on our way. I'll just check Tim's OK . . . '

Tim was still fast asleep so she followed Geoff and Alice into the other cottage. Harry was conscious by this time, propped on a chair in the kitchen. His hands and face were red from the blood oozing from his forehead. He dabbed at the wound with a towel.

Julie went to him. 'Let me look, Harry. What happened?'

'Couple of blokes in balaclavas were banging on the doors and windows. I heard them trampling round the house, so I went out, but they hit me with something. I went out like a light. Next thing I knew they'd gone and Alice was pulling me in here.'

Geoff came in from outside. 'They've made a terrible mess of your garden — plants pulled up, vegetables trampled. Vandals — I know what I'd do with them!'

Julie was tending Harry's wound.. 'You won't need a stitch, at least. I'll clean it up for now, and take you to hospital to have it checked tomorrow.'

Geoff had picked up some papers from the hallway. He looked grim.

'It looks like that assault was meant for us. It's the anti-research brigade. Stupid louts couldn't even target the right house.'

'It was meant for me?' Julie stared in horror at the crudely-written note: *STOP NOW — before it's too late. Target Maldon's, animal killers.*

Julie went to rip it up but Geoff stopped her.

'No, phone the police. And don't touch anything — there could well be loads of clues around.'

'Alice, you and Harry must come and stay with us,' Julie said.

'We can stay at my sister's down the road,' Alice said.

'Tomorrow maybe, but tonight you're coming with us. I need to keep an eye on Harry.' Julie looked at Geoff. 'Will you phone the police?'

Geoff looked white. 'It's only just sinking in — they were aiming for you, Julie. You're not safe — Lord knows what they'll do next.'

⋆ ⋆ ⋆

News of the incident spread quickly round Hemsdale and beyond. It was

250

followed by isolated incidents and vandalism which the police dismissed as copy-cat villainy for the sake of it. Eric Lancaster's car was trashed, some of Maldon's' employees had threatening letters through the post and sinister phone calls. Geoff went back very reluctantly to the States but phoned Julie twice a week and insisted she should rethink her decision about rejoining him, even for a short period until it all simmered down. He was coming back at the end of October for Tim's birthday.

For whatever reason, it was Julie's project that was the main target and Maldon's directors voted unanimously to stop the trials indefinitely.

'That means you're giving in to them,' Julie protested to Eric.

'That doesn't matter. It's not important enough for us to risk our other projects. Sorry, Julie.'

When Olivia telephoned her that evening with her regular pregnancy report, it was she who was doing the cheering up for once.

'I'm sure there'll be lots more projects. It's not as though you've been fired. Tell you what, come over for supper next Saturday; it's ages since you've been round, and with Mum away, too . . .'

'All right, I'd like that. Can I bring Tim?'

There was a fractional pause before Olivia answered, 'Of course. You can't leave him yet, can you?'

'No, though it won't be long. He'll be twelve soon. It makes me feel quite old.'

'Of course you're not, and with Tim growing up, there's plenty of time to spread your wings.'

'What do you mean?'

'Oh, nothing. See you Saturday.'

★   ★   ★

The hold up of her trials was more depressing to Julie than she had expected. It had been going so well, but now she had to contact all her hospitals to stop work on it. She left St Clements till last.

'Hi, Rob, it's Julie — about the trials . . .'

'Yes, I heard. It's a shame but maybe it's for the best. We can pick up later when this blows over. How's your neighbour . . . Mr Lunn, wasn't it?'

'Yes. He's fine, but he and Alice were very shaken up. They're still not back in their cottage.'

'That's sad. Look, I'll let Polly know; she's off sick at the moment.'

'Oh. Is it serious?'

'I'm not sure.' There was a pause before he tentatively asked, 'Has your . . . er . . . Is Geoff still with you?'

'No, he went back last week.'

'So, are you free to come with me to the Shepherd's Crook for dinner?'

'I'd love to.'

'Great. I'm tied up this weekend but I'll ring you to fix a date.'

'I'll look forward to it.'

However Julie was destined to meet Rob sooner than she'd expected. When she and Tim arrived at Pendale Court on Saturday, Robert Kendall greeted them as well as Olivia and Michael.

'Surprise!' Olivia laughed delightedly. 'Rob came to see Mike about some finance thing and I've persuaded him to stay for supper.'

'Oh.' Julie wished she'd taken a bit more trouble with her appearance. 'That's nice. Tim, you remember Rob?'

'Yep. We played snooker at Aunt Olivia's Midsummer party.'

'Yes, and you pretty well beat me up. Is it all right if we have a rematch, Mike?'

'Sure. I'll come too. Have we time before supper, Olivia?'

'Loads of time. Off you go.'

The sisters wandered out into the garden.

'There's bags of time. Ellena's cooking up something complicated.

Don't you think Rob is a lovely man?'

'I suppose. Olivia, did you set this up?'

'Who, me? Would I do such a thing? Mike simply mentioned that Rob was coming to talk business so I invited him for supper. Do you mind?'

'Not at all. You're looking very well. No problems?'

Olivia shook her head. 'No. I'm so excited, Ju!' She put her hands on her swelling stomach. 'Not long now.'

'End of October, isn't it?'

'More mid-October, we think. I'm so happy about it I can hardly bear it. Nothing must go wrong.'

'It won't.'

The evening was such a success that Olivia wanted to arrange another one. Mike looked worried when she suggested a full day out visiting a local beauty spot.

'There's a new garden centre opened the other side of Branston Moor. It's a lovely drive. Except for Tim's welcome party, I've hardly moved out of the house. We could take a picnic! Rob, could you come with us?'

'If I'm not on call.'

Mike still looked dubious. 'What do you think, Rob?'

'There's certainly no harm in a drive out. Olivia's doing well, but it's your decision.'

'In the olden days, women used to drop their babies in the fields and carry on working,' Tim announced in a matter-of-fact way. 'We did it in social history.'

'And the mortality rate for infant deaths and their mothers was pretty high. I wouldn't recommend it,' Rob said.

'So that's settled, is it?' Olivia's eyes were sparkling. 'Next Sunday, we'll meet here around eleven o'clock. Picnic lunch. We'll take the four-by-four, put in rugs, chairs, and go right out on to the moors for the picnic, then we'll take in the new house and gardens.'

'Only if you're up to it.' Michael put his arm round his wife, 'Let's see what the weather's like and how you feel.'

'The weather's supposed to be fair for the week, with more lovely autumn sunshine. And just think, our next outing could be with our new addition, carry-cots, nappies, bottles. It'll be such fun, won't it, Mike?'

'I certainly hope so. We've waited long enough.' He pulled her to him and kissed her.

Going home in the car Tim asked whether his new cousin-to-be had a name yet.

'I don't think so. Olivia's superstitious about that, she thinks it's tempting fate.'

'Mmm. You don't mind if I don't come next Sunday, do you? I've got football trials. Uncle Eddie's taking me to the sports field and then out for a pizza afterwards.'

'Oh, when was that arranged?'

'Ages ago. You know Uncle Ed's nuts about football. He thinks I've got potential. So does Dad.'

'Oh. Good.' Julie could feel Tim

moving away from her into a male world. It was good that he had two uncles.

'Mum — ' he yawned ' — would you like a baby?'

'What? Not at the moment, thanks. I've enough on my plate and I'm quite happy with what I've got.'

'That's good. I wonder how Granny's getting on?' He yawned again, 'Mum, I like Robert, he's ace. I beat him at snooker again.'

A few minutes later, when Julie glanced at him, he was fast asleep. She smiled tenderly. I'm very lucky to have such a son, she thought.

★   ★   ★

The sunny September spell held and on the Sunday before her mother was due back from France, Julie drove over to Pendale Court. Rob had phoned her in the week to make a date for the Shepherd's Crook and to confirm Sunday. Her spirits rose as she swung into Olivia's drive.

Rob was already there, helping to load up the 4×4, and the dogs were going wild, recognising an outing. Rob greeted her with a kiss. She was glad she'd splashed out on her new trousers and top. Her hair was loose around her face today and a light tan gave her skin a healthy glow.

Rob took her hand. 'You look lovely.'

Olivia came out of the house carrying a small picnic basket.

'It's just a few extras. We've got the main hamper in the back of the car. Isn't it a glorious, day? Aren't you glad we planned this?'

Mike, looking anxious, came to join them. 'Are you sure about this?' he asked his wife. 'You had a pretty restless night.'

'I'm fine. I didn't sleep too well — the baby was kicking, that's all. Don't fuss, I've been looking forward to this all week. Let's go.'

The suburb of Royston soon gave way to a mixture of farmland, open moorland and woodland.

'Where are we making for, Olivia?' Mike asked.

Olivia was absorbed in her map. 'I'd like to go up the Ames Crag. You remember it, Julie? We used to go there with Mum and Dad when you were a baby. It's way up over the moors. There's a rocky outcrop, a sort of monolithic stone, a ring of pillars — perfect for a picnic. The view at the top's spectacular. Keep on this road, Mike, there should be a turn off.'

'It's more a track than a road.' Mike braked sharply as a couple of sheep wandered across the track and the vehicle bucked and bumped.

'It's lovely country anyway,' Olivia said almost half an hour later.

'I think we're going round in circles,' Mike said. 'Do you know where we are, Rob?'

'I'm not sure. I can't recall coming up here. Let's see the map, Olivia.'

The landscape was changing. It was harsher, bleaker, and with hardly any cars. There wasn't a soul to be seen.

Rob pored over the map. 'I think we're miles from Ames Crag — it's right on the other side of the moor.

'We're lost then,' Mike said.

'Not really, we've just wandered off course a bit,' said Rob. 'If we take the next left turning, there should be an intersection.'

'I'm feeling peckish,' Mike said. 'Why don't we find a picnic spot around here and assess the situation.'

'If we go on a bit farther, there should be somewhere a few miles on.'

Five miles along, the track widened and there was a left turn. 'Down there,' Rob directed. 'It's quite high up and there are some boulders and flat rocks. It's a good spot.'

'But we're still lost?' Mike was worried.

'No — I'll check the ordnance survey map. It's time for lunch anyway.'

'Rob.' Julie nudged him. 'Olivia's been quiet for ages and she's sort of bent over. I thought she was dozing but . . . '

A soon as the car stopped, Rob leapt out of his seat and round to Olivia in the front.

'Olivia,' he said sharply, 'sit up. What's wrong?'

'I don't know, I just felt . . . very strange.'

'Let's get you out, walk about a bit. Any pain?'

'No. I had some last night but it was gone in the morning . . . *Aah!* Yes, just then.' Olivia clutched Rob's hand.

'Here, step down. Careful — ' Gently he led her out of the vehicle.

By now Julie and Michael were out of the car and Michael put his arm round Olivia. 'I told you we shouldn't have come. We'll get you home straight away.'

'Just let me look at her,' Rob said calmly, 'If she's going into labour we've plenty of time. If it's a false start, there's no problem anyway.'

'*Ow!*' Olivia doubled up again. 'It is . . . the baby's coming — I know it is.' She looked panic-stricken. 'It's just like last time.'

'No, it isn't,' Julie said. 'Last time the baby was premature — you're too far on for that this time. Come on, Olly, you're lucky to have two professionals here. Mike, get the rugs out of the car, and cushions . . . '

'I can't give birth out here,' Olivia wailed.

'It's a lovely spot, keep your eyes on the view. Your baby's going to be proud of you when it grows up. A nature birth.' Gently Rob and Julie lowered Olivia on to the rug.

'*Aah!*' Olivia shrieked. 'The water's have broken.'

'OK, that's fine. Now let me examine you. Mike, rig up a kind of shelter here — I think I saw a tarpaulin in the back of the car. Then come and hold her hand.'

Rob examined Olivia, while Julie knelt on the other side, her eyes fixed on Rob. He looked very intent as he put his ear to Olivia's tummy, and it seemed an age before he said calmly,

'Mike, you need to call the air ambulance.'

'What's wrong?'

'Just call it, tell them the baby's in transverse lie, there's a cord prolapse — got that? They'll know what to bring. Move, Mike.'

'I'm going to lose my baby again!' Olivia wailed.

'No, you're not,' Rob said forcefully. 'The only trouble is you may deliver the baby before the ambulance arrives.' He didn't dare tell her the baby's heartbeat was too slow — but Julie's face told him that she knew what he was thinking. 'Don't push yet . . . '

'I can't stop . . . ' Olivia gasped.

'Deep breaths,' Julie said. 'The ambulance is on its way.'

Mike came running back. 'Good grief, it *is* coming, isn't it?'

'Very likely . . . I just need . . . there . . . now, Olivia, you can push now. Mike, we need warm things to wrap the baby in . . . ah, here he comes.'

Finally Olivia delivered her little boy

into Rob's waiting hands.

'Julie, quickly — I need something to tie off the cord.'

'He's not breathing,' she whispered.

'Why doesn't he cry? He's dead, isn't he?' Olivia struggled to sit up.

Rob was breathing into the baby's mouth, gently tapping his heart.

'He's blue,' Julie murmured. 'Rob?'

'No, he'll be fine — look, he's already pinking up. And listen to that.'

A few convulsive grunts were followed by the outraged cry of the new-born.

Rob took off his T-shirt which was warm from the sun on his body and wrapped the child in it, then in the soft jumper that Julie gave him.

'Here you are, Olivia — your son, making a dramatic entrance into the world.'

'Rob, thank you. What can I say?'

'Shall I cancel the helicopter?' Mike asked.

'No, it'll have set off — and baby and mother need monitoring,' Rob said. 'It was so very quick, I'd like to see them in hospital as soon as possible. I wouldn't fancy that bumpy road across the moors — that's probably what shook the baby on his way.'

Within fifteen minutes, the helicopter had arrived, bringing a paramedic. Mother and baby were soon safely on board too, and Mike followed, turning as he climbed in to mouth 'thank you', before the door closed and the helicopter swung away towards the hospital.

'Wow!' Julie was shaking.

Rob put his arms round her and held her tight. 'Close call,' he said, 'the heartbeat was fading.'

Julie shivered. 'Don't think about it.'

'I think we need to take a moment. Hot coffee?'

'Please. Rob, you were absolutely wonderful.'

'Sshh.' He laid a finger on her lips. 'I'm pleased to be of service to the Balboni family — at any time.'

He took her in his arms and kissed her, and they clung together for a long time, relief and happiness seeping through them.

Then he let her go, looked into her eyes and said huskily, 'I'm falling in love with you, Julie. A thing I never thought I'd do again.'

'Rob . . .'

'No, don't say anything yet. It's been quite a day; let's come back down to earth and see what Ellena's put in this hamper. I'm starving!'

The Man For Julie

'Isn't he the most beautiful child you've ever seen?' Olivia cradled her son as she showed him off to his new family.

'Unique, I'd say.' Julie gazed wistfully at the sleeping baby.

'A miracle,' Sandra breathed, touching the soft cheek. 'A Yorkshire baby born on a Yorkshire moor in double-quick time.'

'I'm sure I started the previous night,' Olivia said, 'but then it sort of stopped so I thought it was a false alarm — and I didn't want to miss the outing.'

'You almost frightened me to death.' Julie shuddered. 'But then, you always were a drama queen!'

They were at Olivia's house in the nursery, the baby a week old and thriving. Already his birth was family legend, embellished with each telling.

To Julie, it also marked the moment Rob had told her he loved her.

'Have you decided on a name yet?' Sandra queried.

'Yes. It was easy — Matthew Michael Robert.'

'Robert?' Julie echoed.

'For Robert Kendall. But for him Matthew might not have made it. We're going to ask him to be one of his godfathers.'

'Does he know?'

'We've only just decided.'

'I'm seeing him tonight, shall I tell him?'

Both women's eyes swivelled from baby to Julie.

'You are?' they exclaimed together.

'It's only for supper, it's no big deal.'

'You don't have to explain.' Olivia smiled at her mother. 'We're not nosy, are we, Mum?'

'Not a bit,' Sandra lied.

'You can tell Rob about the name,' Olivia said, 'but Mike and I will do the godparent bit.'

Julie wandered around the room reading the congratulations cards.

''All love and best wishes from Carlo and family'. Did you tell him? I meant to.'

Olivia nodded. 'It was the right thing to do. Matthew is Carlo's grandson, after all. Mum, do you mind?'

'I'm delighted. As I've said before, I've wasted too many years on bitterness. It's time to look forward.'

'You certainly look well. Your trip to France did you good.'

'We're going again in the spring — advanced courses this time.'

Olivia frowned. 'I hope you're planning to save some granny time for this little chap, because Matthew Power is a top priority from now on.'

'Don't you worry, I'll granny him to death!'

★　★　★

At the Shepherd's Crook that evening Julie and Rob sat at an alcove table in the cosy dining-room, fussed over by Martha and Nicky.

'I'm so glad to see you both,' Martha beamed. 'How's your dad, Rob?'

'Not too good, I'm afraid. I'm going to see him next week.'

'You'll miss the big Maldon's event then?'

'I'll try to be back for that.'

The food was delicious, and the evening went swiftly. Julie and Rob talked as good friends do, but both were vividly aware of the stronger feelings binding them together.

Later, Rob drove home slowly, reluctant to end the evening. On the outskirts of Hemsdale, he pulled into a layby and turned to Julie.

'Thank you for a wonderful evening.' He drew her to him and kissed her. 'I meant what I said last Sunday — I love you, Julie. I want to be with you all the time.'

'Rob, I don't know. I'm scared — last time I made such a mistake . . . '

'You were young, and we've both

been in love before. You were . . . in love with Geoff?'

'Yes, I was, and I still like him very much. And of course there's Tim.'

'He's important, I know that.'

Rob kissed her and she clung to him, feeling her heart pound, her body melt to his. She was almost lost until she forced herself to break away.

'Geoff wants me to go back to America with him,' she blurted out.

'Oh.' There was a long pause. 'And do you want to go?'

She shook her head. 'Of course not, but Tim needs a father.'

Rob moved away from her and switched on the ignition.

'You need time to think about the future, to make a choice. I'll phone you from London and I'll try to get back for the Maldon's party.'

* * *

The second part of Maldon's' 25th anniversary celebrations was to be a big family event, timed to take place the weekend the clocks went back for the end of British summer time. There was to be a barbecue, fireworks display and bonfire. A computer games centre was also being set up with competitions for the children, old and young.

The following day was also Tim's twelfth birthday and Geoff had promised to pay a flying visit.

Rob phoned Julie most days, and on the days that he didn't she missed him. There was no doubt where her heart lay, but Tim was thrilled his father was coming over for his birthday. He had settled in well at secondary school, making new friends. Would Geoff's visit, with his reminders of sunny California, unsettle him, Julie worried.

As if to underline the contrast, the Saturday morning of the party dawned with grey skies and misty drizzle. Geoff had arrived late on Friday might and was staying in Sandra's ground-floor flat since she was away. Tim had woken early and gone down to see him.

Julie was in bed and still asleep when her son prodded her awake.

'He's here, Mum; we're making breakfast downstairs. It's nearly ready so get up. I've made pancakes . . .'

She groaned. 'It's Saturday, Tim. I don't have to get up so early.'

'But Dad's here!'

Julie sighed. 'OK, give me a few minutes.'

She went down in her dressing-gown but they were already tucking into bacon, scrambled eggs and pancakes.

Geoff stood up and kissed her. 'You look lovely, Julie.'

'Mmm. Good flight? Just one pancake for me, thanks, Tim.'

Geoff resumed his breakfast. 'Any more trouble from those saboteurs?'

'No, all quiet so far. We may restart the trials.'

'I'm not happy to hear that. You'd be a lot safer in California.'

Tim looked up, surprised. 'Are you — are we . . . ?'

'No.' Julie was very firm. 'We're not

going to California.' She glared at Geoff. 'Tim's happy at his new school, aren't you, Tim?'

'Yes, but . . .'

'So everything's fine. Perhaps I will have another pancake. They're scrumptious.'

Geoff and Tim went into town during the day to buy Tim's birthday present, while Julie caught up with some work. Rob hadn't phoned, so she guessed he probably wouldn't make the party. She worried for him about his father.

In the early evening Geoff drove Julie, Tim and Liam, Tim's invited guest, to Maldon's. Fields near the main buildings had been commandeered for a parking lot and the erection of a large marquee. Powerful arc lights cut through the gathering dusk. A huge bonfire was ready to be lit and food and drinks were already being served in the marquee. A loudspeaker relayed music. A room in the buildings had been set up for the

275

computer games competition.

'What a crush,' Geoff said, as they made their way to the marquee. 'I saw your friends Dan and Val in the car park, and that Polly woman, the one who came to the cottage. Half of Hemsdale's here!'

'Very likely — the directors wanted to make it a community event.'

'Looks like a success on that count. You wait here, I'll try to make my way in and get burgers and chips for the boys. Where are they?'

'Over there with some friends. I'll call them over. The fireworks should be starting soon.'

'OK, shan't be long. I hope.'

Julie was about to call the boys when a touch on her shoulder made her spin round, straight into Rob's arms.

'Rob! I didn't expect you. Your father . . . ?'

'He's just about holding on. I'll have to go back but I . . . I had to see you, I missed you.'

Tim and Liam joined them just as Geoff emerged with armfuls of take-away boxes which he nearly dropped when he saw Rob. For a few awkward moments there was silence, only broken as the first fireworks whooshed upwards and the night sky blazed into diamond-studded brilliance.

After a while Tim and Liam became restless.

'Mum, can we go to the computer room now? We're due to meet the guys there. We'll be back later for the barbecue.'

'But . . .'

'See ya, Mum,' and they were gone.

Rob went to get drinks and the three of them found a bench to sit on near the bonfire, now fully alight.

'How long are you staying in Hemsdale?' he asked Geoff.

'I'm not sure, I'll see how things go,' Geoff said, glancing at Julie. 'I thought you were in London.'

'I was.'

The two men were polite but Julie

was uncomfortably aware of the tension between them.

The fireworks were building to a grand finale.

'Maybe we should look for the boys,' Julie fretted.

'They'll be battling it out in the games . . . ' He broke off. 'What was that?'

The blast of an explosion drowned out the crackle and pop of the fireworks. The display had reached a crescendo, and everyone was gazing skywards, assuming the noise was part of the finale.

'I'm going to find the boys,' Julie said. 'They're in the conference room, I think.'

'No,' Rob interrupted, 'there was a change of plan. I heard it on the loudspeaker as I came in — laboratory number three.'

People were beginning to move across the field towards the barbecue when there was a static crackle from the loudspeakers and Eric Lancaster's voice broke through. 'I'm afraid there's been an . . . an accident in one of the labs we were using a computer games room — an explosion. The fire brigade is on its way.'

Julie clutched her heart. 'Tim! He's in there . . . '

'Where is it?' Geoff said urgently. 'Julie . . . the lab, show me.'

'I know,' Rob said, 'we had a tour. Come on.'

Now there was a rising sense of panic. If there had been one explosion, there may be another. Eric called for calm.

'Nobody's hurt, everyone please stay where you are . . . '

'Nevertheless, people surged towards the car park and main buildings.

There was a collective gasp from the crowd as another smaller bang rang out and at the same time smoke and flames began to curl through the shattered windows.

Geoff, Julie and Rob were ahead of the crowd and had reached the main entrance. Julie screamed Tim's name as she raced up the stairs.

'Why aren't they coming out?' she shouted.

'Down here!' Rob ran down the corridor where smoke was curling about the floor.

A small group of bewildered people were being shepherded out of the buildings.

'Did you say lab three, Rob? In there!' Julie pointed. As she spoke there were several more explosions.

'Chemicals — what idiot . . . ?'

'Never mind. Tim? Tim, are you in there?' she shouted as she pushed against the door — but it wouldn't open. 'Tim, Liam — open the door.'

'We've tried. It's stuck.' There was fear in their voices.

'It's the new locks! They've clicked shut. It's the new security system, you can't break in.' Julie tried to keep her voice calm. 'Tim, what's happening in there? How many of you are there?'

'About a dozen. There's a fire at one

end . . . smoke . . . ' He coughed. 'Fumes . . . choking us . . . please . . . help . . . '

'Keep calm, Tim. Try the windows. It should be easy — they won't be locked. Hurry, Tim!'

It seemed an agonisingly long wait but in fact was only seconds before Tim cried out, 'Yes, we've got two open — but we're on the second floor.'

'I know it's quite a drop but you've no choice. We'll catch you.'

Geoff and Rob were already running back, shouting at her to follow.

'No, I'll stay here,' she responded. She couldn't leave her son.

'OK, Mum, we'll climb out,' came Tim's voice through the door. 'But there are some smaller boys and they're scared.'

'All right — just hang on. There are people outside. Your dad and Rob are probably already there. Be brave, Tim. Line up the boys.'

'Mum, Liam's forced another window. He says there are people down there with blankets. I'm going to climb up . . .'

'Be careful, Tim!' she called.

She pressed her ear to the door, desperately trying to hear what was going on. She heard scuffling and yelling . . . then somebody cried out in pain . . .

'Tim!' Her voice cracked with terror.

'Mrs Haywood?' It was Liam's voice, faint and shaking. 'Tim's fallen off the window-ledge. He's hurt his leg — I think maybe he's broken his ankle. The fire's worse in here now . . .' He gasped and coughed.

'Liam, go to the window and yell for all you're worth. Yell for help. And, Liam, if you can, drag Tim towards the window. I'm coming.'

The smoke was thickening in the corridor. Julie shielded her nose and mouth with her arm, and ran.

'Tim, Tim, please be all right. I'll go to America if that's what you want . . . anything . . . just be safe.'

She reached the entrance just as all

the lights went out. Missing her footing, she stumbled and fell. She tried to get back on her feet, but pain shot through her ankle.

Desperately, painfully, she dragged herself out of the building. In the distance she could hear the yowling sirens of the approaching fire engines.

Looking back at the building, she could see the flames were spreading and black smoke was billowing out of the laboratories. And then, miraculously, she could see a long ladder being manoeuvred into position to reach the windows. There were knots of people clustered below, all looking upwards.

Again she tried to stand, and fell.

A figure came running, yelling: 'Julie, Julie, it's OK, they're safe . . . '

She willed herself to stand, but the pain was sickening and she collapsed. As she blacked out, she heard Rob repeating, 'He's safe, Tim's safe, no-one's hurt. Julie . . . ' and she was in his arms.

Coincidentally both Tim and Julie

had fractured ankles and the evening ended with them both in St Clements' accident and emergency department. Ankles strapped, they shared a small side ward.

By now Julie had learned that Eric Lancaster had orchestrated the boys' rescue before the firemen arrived. Liam had followed the other boys, jumping into blankets held open by men below, and Geoff had climbed the ladder to bring Tim to safety in the nick of time. Minutes later the laboratory had been consumed by flames.

Geoff sat between the two beds, pale and distressed, cracking his knuckles endlessly, his eyes on Tim.

'I was really scared, Dad,' Tim said in a small voice, 'especially when I fell off the window-ledge. I had to hop. Liam helped me . . . '

'You're safe now, and that's how I'm keeping you, don't worry.' He turned to Julie. 'See? You have to come back with me now — it's just not safe here.'

Julie wearily turned her head. 'It

could happen in the States too. Accidents happen anywhere.'

'This was no accident. This was someone deliberately blowing up the laboratory.' Geoff frowned. 'I'm not risking it,' he insisted. 'I shall seek custody through the courts if you won't come.'

'There's no need for that, Geoff. I'll leave Maldon's and go back to nursing.'

Geoff took her hand. 'No. Make a home with us in California — me and Tim. I love you, Julie, and I want to keep you both safe.'

Reaction was setting in fast, and as tears streamed down her cheeks, she remembered her promise: 'anything — I'll go to America', trading the promise for her boy's safety. Would she now have to keep her side of the bargain?

Suddenly she was unbelievably tired, too tired to think — or care. Let Geoff take charge . . .

'Oh, all right, whatever you say.' With a last look at her boy, safe no thanks to her, she closed her eyes.

Geoff kissed her and went to Tim.

'It's all settled, Tim. We're going back to the States. I'll book our flights. I'm not leaving without you and Mum.'

'Dad — ' Tim, too, was struggling against sleep. 'You could have asked me what I want,' he said as his eyes closed.

★ ★ ★

The police started their investigation immediately and Geoff refused to go back to the States until the culprits were found. He had business in the northern towns and could stay indefinitely before he took Tim and Julie back with him.

Once home, a great lethargy stole over Julie and a broken ankle was a good excuse to burrow under the duvet and shut out the world. Tim made a much faster recovery, enjoyed a brief fame as a hero and was soon back at school, adeptly hopping around the playground with the aid of his crutches.

Rob had had to leave for Seaford immediately because his father was still extremely ill; sadly, he died a few days later. He talked to Julie most days but he was distracted by family affairs and couldn't leave Seaford until after the funeral.

A week after the disaster Eric Lancaster telephoned Julie.

'How are you? We miss you.'

'I'm sorry, I'm not ready . . .'

'No, no, that's not what I'm phoning about. May I call round this evening? The police . . . well .. There have been startling developments. It's not public yet but I'm allowed to tell you, in the circumstances. How's young Tim?'

'Fighting fit! The young mend much more easily.'

'I'm glad he's up and about. I'll call in after work then, shall I?'

'That'll be fine.'

Sandra had taken charge of the cooking and Geoff and Tim had practically moved into her part of the house. For the moment that suited

Julie, who was still consumed by guilt about Tim.

Geoff insisted on being there when Eric called. Eric looked surprised to see him but greeted him warmly.

'I shan't keep you but I know Julie's been fretting about what happened to Tim. I hear you're all thinking of leaving us and going to live in California.'

'We are. I've booked us open flight tickets for San Diego as soon as she's fit.'

'It's not decided,' Julie said.

'Is one of the reasons for taking Julie away the fear of further action by — ?'

'They'll strike again, mark my words,' Geoff burst in.

'I don't think so. You see, the police have caught the culprits and they don't belong to any group — certainly not any animal rights group. They're lone operators: one leader, and one deluded follower.'

'What . . . ?'

'I hate to tell you, Julie, but it was

Polly Fellowes — or rather, her boyfriend, Gary Wilkes, who caused the explosions.'

Julie gasped. 'Polly? But that's impossible! Why would she? She's a brilliant doctor . . . '

'That's as may be, but she has psychiatric problems, and had also come under the unfortunate influence of this guy Wilkes. The police have suspected them for a while, but after the fire, Polly confessed. Wilkes fled the country, leaving her to face the music.'

'I can't believe it! Polly! But why? How could she?'

'She was horrified by what happened. She told the police that Wilkes had intended a minor explosion in the lab. Neither of them had any idea the lab was to be used as a computer games room. That was a last-minute arrangement that had only come about when something went wrong with the circuitry and the boffins couldn't fix it so it was hurriedly removed to lab three — with hindsight, a bad idea.'

'Actually I feel sorry for Polly, she's had some bad deals in her life,' Julie said sadly.

'Apparently she was completely under Wilkes's control,' Eric said. 'And I hate to tell you this but she deeply resented being passed over for Rob. She'd set her heart on the senior consultant post. So as far as she was concerned, the chance to ruin your drug trials was an added inducement to fall in with Wilkes's plan. She'll be arrested and bailed pending psychiatric reports.'

Eric turned to Geoff. 'So you see, this was a one-off, not a planned campaign of violence, although I believe Wilkes has a grudge against pharmaceutical companies in general — due to some family history which will doubtless emerge in court.'

Geoff was doubtful. '*If* they find him.'

'I'm sure the police will catch up with him,' Eric assured him. 'Julie, if you do rejoin us — and I really hope you do — I think we can safely say that Maldon's will be trouble free and the publicity accruing from this case will prove we do not do animal experiments.'

Julie was still in some degree of shock. 'For Polly to ruin her own hard work — it's unbelievable.'

'I agree, but that's another story.'

At last Eric, already late home, hurried away, pleading a dinner engagement.

★   ★   ★

'It doesn't alter anything, Julie,' Geoff said. 'I still want you to come to the States. You promised.'

'I know I did, but I was under terrible emotional pressure . . . and at the time I was so relieved to have Tim safe that I'd have promised anything to anybody. I'm sorry.'

Geoff could see his future slipping away from him again.

'You must give it another chance

— for Tim's sake.'

'No, I can't.' She sighed wearily. 'I like you, Geoff. You're a lovely, wonderful dad and you can see Tim all you like — but I don't love you.'

'You could, in time. You did once,' he persisted.

'Oh, Geoff, I did love you, but I was so young. I was flattered. You were the good handsome sociable guy. I lacked confidence and I thought I could hide behind you. But I couldn't fit the role you had planned for me — the corporate wife just wasn't me.'

She stroked his cheek gently. 'You'll always be in my heart, Geoff. We're Tim's parents — it's a strong bond. I wouldn't have missed out on our marriage, but let's keep it as a good memory and still be friends for Tim's sake.'

'I've fallen in love with you all over again — deeper, too,' Geoff said sadly. 'Isn't there the faintest chance?'

'I was briefly tempted, after the fire,' she conceded, 'but it just wouldn't work.'

'Why not?' He looked bewildered.

'Because I'm in love with someone else,' she told him simply. She hadn't meant to say it, but it was true — and now she couldn't wait to say it to Rob.

'Oh.' He was quiet for a minute.

'I suppose it's Rob Kendall. If I'm honest, I'd guessed as much, but I didn't want to face it. And he loves you?'

'He says so. I haven't told him I . . .'

'You should. Right away. Ring him.'

'He's in Seaford.'

'And don't they have phones in Seaford?' His lips twitched slightly.

'Oh, Geoff!' Julie flung her arms around him. 'Thank you. We'll always be friends, won't we?'

'We will. I'm taking Tim to play football now. Phone Rob — lucky man. I'll fly home tomorrow.'

An hour later, when Sandra went upstairs to check on Julie, her daughter was holding the phone, eyes faraway and dreamy, her face smiling.

'Er . . . good news, Julie?'

'Yes. Mum — Robert and I are getting married. He's just asked me.'

'And you said yes?'

'I did — subject to Tim's approval.'

★ ★ ★

On a splendid golden day in November, Robert and Julie were married at Hemsdale Manor, a popular local wedding venue. It was a small gathering, strictly family and friends; the couple had no wish to upstage Sam and Jane's wedding the following month.

Carlo Balboni, bursting with happy pride, led his daughter towards her bridegroom.

As Rob and Julie took their solemn vows, the aura of love and commitment was so tangible that there were many handkerchiefs dabbing at moist eyes.

At the lunch-time reception, Carlo spoke of his great joy at meeting his English family and hoped there would be many such occasions to bind the two families.

Much fuss was made of baby Matthew, who was already showing signs of his Italian heritage with his thick dark hair and Balboni eyes. Young Bianca and Angelo, shy at first, attached themselves to Tim, who adopted a proprietorial air and introduced them to all the guests as 'my Italian cousins from Florence.'

A surprise highlight of the day was Sandra Balboni looking youthful and slim in a suit of autumn colours and a cream velvet hat. She introduced the handsome grey-haired man at her side as Jean-Pierre Mountjoy, owner of Chateau du Foret in Southern France.

'A very good friend of mine,' she announced airily to her rather startled children.

Jean-Pierre took her hand and kissed it, his eloquent eyes telling them he hoped in the future to be more than just a good friend.

It was early evening before Julie and Rob were able to leave for a brief honeymoon in London. Changed for the journey, Julie looked for Tim. He was with the Balboni children, chatting earnestly, picking up Italian phrases.

'Hi, Mum. You look nice.'

'Thank you. We're off in a few minutes. You OK?'

'Sure. Grandpa Carlos and Isabella are staying here at the Manor for a few days. I'm going to show them around.'

'You're sure . . . about . . . Rob and me?'

'It's a bit late if I'm not!' He spluttered with laughter. 'Mum, we talked about it when you got engaged to Rob — it's cool. I'm dead lucky to have two homes, three if you count Florence, two dads — well, one real dad but Rob's OK. We'll get along fine. So stop worrying.'

'Thanks. I love you.' She hugged him.

'Love you too. Isn't it time you were leaving?'

Rob and Julie left Hemsdale in a shower of good wishes, confetti, and tin cans on the car's bumper tied on by

Eddie and Sam.

Once clear of the Manor Rob stopped to remove the tin cans.

Back in the car he drew his new bride into his arms and kissed her lingeringly.

'That was a brilliant send-off, and we're going to have a brilliant life. I love you, Julie, and I always will.'

Full of happiness, Julie kissed him back.

'I know, Rob. We've come a long way from Fletcher Comprehensive and this is just the beginning.'

THE END

We do hope that you have enjoyed reading this large print book.

Did you know that all of our titles are available for purchase?

We publish a wide range of high quality large print books including:
Romances, Mysteries, Classics
General Fiction
Non Fiction and Westerns

Special interest titles available in large print are:
The Little Oxford Dictionary
Music Book, Song Book
Hymn Book, Service Book

Also available from us courtesy of Oxford University Press:
Young Readers' Dictionary
(large print edition)
Young Readers' Thesaurus
(large print edition)

For further information or a free brochure, please contact us at:
Ulverscroft Large Print Books Ltd.,
The Green, Bradgate Road, Anstey,
Leicester, LE7 7FU, England.
Tel: (00 44) 0116 236 4325
Fax: (00 44) 0116 234 0205